Selected by
Hugh MacDiarmid

Penguin Books

Penguin Books Ltd, Harmondsworth,
Middlesex, England
Penguin Books Inc., 7110 Ambassador Road,
Baltimore, Maryland 21207, U.S.A.
Penguin Books Australia Ltd, Ringwood,
Victoria, Australia

First published 1973
Selection copyright © Penguin Books Ltd, 1973
Introduction copyright © C. M. Grieve, 1973

Made and printed in Great Britain by
Richard Clay (The Chaucer Press) Ltd,
Bungay, Suffolk
Set in Monotype Ehrhardt

Poet to Poet
Henryson Selected by Hugh MacDiarmid

ROBERT HENRYSON (fl. 1480) was a Middle Scots poet
best known for *The Testament of Cresseid* and *The Fables
of Aesop*. Almost nothing is known about his life except
that he was a schoolteacher in Fife and was dead by
about 1506.

HUGH MACDIARMID, pseudonym of Christopher
Murray Grieve, was born in Langholm in 1892. He is a
poet, journalist, critic, founder of the Scottish
Renaissance movement, and a member of the
Communist Party. His reputation was established in the
twenties when he launched a passionate polemic against
the prevailing cultural situation in Scotland at that time,
through periodicals, books, poems and articles. He
writes in Scots and English, and his use of Scots has
helped it develop into the creatively expressive language
of some of the best Scottish poetry today. He is the most
important Scottish poet of this century. The first
comprehensive selection of his poetry to appear in
England was published in Penguins in 1970.

HENRYSON

Contents

Introduction

Who is the greatest of Scottish poets? In asking that question we will leave Gaelic poets out of account, though both Duncan ban McIntyre and Alastair MacMhaigstir Alastair (Alexander MacDonald) would deserve to be considered in any comprehensive view, and so also perhaps would the two Latin poets, George Buchanan and Arthur Johnstone. When the contemporary Scottish Renaissance Movement was launched in the twenties of this century it was immediately realized that to get Scottish poetry out of the doldrums into which it had fallen after the death of Burns and restore it to a level worthy of the international prestige it had enjoyed in the fifteenth and sixteenth centuries in the work of such great makars as Robert Henryson, William Dunbar, Sir David Lyndsay, and Gavin Douglas, it was necessary for the work of these men to be much better known and for the slough of despond into which our once great tradition had fallen – an apparently bottomless abyss of doggerel, moralistic rubbish, mawkish sentimentality and witless jocosity – to be once again transcended. So the movement proceeded under the slogan 'Not Burns – Dunbar!' and rapidly achieved successes in all the three languages used by Scottish writers: Scots (or, as Burns called it, Lallans), Gaelic and English, sufficient to rank the past forty to fifty years as one of the richest in our literary history.

'Not Burns – Dunbar!' The choice of Dunbar was an obvious one, but not necessarily the right one. Dunbar was a great technician of verse and had language at large. From certain angles his work seemed surprisingly modern. It appealed to the taste of many young poets in a way that the work of the other great makars failed to do. But this was a

transitional phase. The necessity *reculer pour mieux sauter*
could not be denied. Burns, let alone his successors, had to be
almost wholly repudiated in this connection. But that Dunbar
should be singled out as the great exemplar in the first flush of
a movement that was, as John Buchan put it, both revolution-
ary and reactionary was natural enough, but not necessarily
the best and final choice. He was better known than the
others and his work was more easily accessible. But second
thoughts have emphasized the greater importance of Henryson who, it is safe to say, was in nobody's mind at the time
and is still far from generally appreciated. Where Henryson
was known at all, the facts that he was a schoolmaster and a
moralist were against him. It did not seem likely that he
would prove congenial in the climate of our time. We had had
far too much moralizing and didacticism. Dr M. M. Gray, in
her *Scottish Poetry from Barbour to James VI* (London, Dent,
1935) rightly maintains that

Henryson alone, in poetry other than lyric, approaches in his
subjects and character the high seriousness of great poetry. He
presents tragic situations and characters stirred by deep feelings, he
creates moving and pathetic speeches, he alone seems to have been
able to infuse into the new poetry some of the passion and tragedy
of the ballad, and thus to create something individual in his
Testament of Cresseid and his *Orpheus and Eurydice*. He also has a
more genial humour, and a power of giving very real and animated
representation to everyday things, as in *The Fables*. He has more
creative power; he is, to use the old Scottish word, a greater *makar*
than the others.

Mr H. Harvey Wood, in his essay on Henryson in *Edinburgh Essays on Scots Literature* (Edinburgh and London,
1933), says:

Until 1865, Henryson was known only by *Robene and Makyne*
and the *Testament of Cresseid*, when he was known at all. *The
Fables, Orpheus and Eurydice, The Bludy Serk, The Annunciation*

were little known, and are little known to this day – shabby treatment for the greatest, without equal, of the Scots Makars. Dunbar,
who is the only other worthy of comparison, was a more brilliant
technician, and greater virtuoso, one of the most original metrists,
not only in Scots but in all English literature. But Henryson's
equipment, though never obtrusive, was always adequate to his
own purposes, and his purposes were more poetic purposes than
those of Dunbar. He is never a mere virtuoso, and his originality is
not of the obvious kind of Dunbar's – yet he is, essentially, the
more original poet of the two. His originality is of the kind that
places a poet in the main current of poetic development; Dunbar's
is one of turbulent and technical eccentricity.

When I invented and published the slogan 'Not Burns –
Dunbar!', like most Scots of my age I had come late and quite
inadequately to a knowledge of the makars. We were taught
nothing of them in our schools and colleges. We realized at
the outset the necessity *épater les Anglais* and the choice of
Dunbar was shocking enough. It is only since then, and as a
result of our Movement, that Scottish literature is now
taught in all our universities (though there is still no chair in
the subject) both in the ordinary and honours classes, and an
increasing number of students are now actually graduating in
the subject. In our schools too the pupils get a good deal more
Scots poetry than we did in the first decade of the century.
So with hindsight I can now wish that in the early twenties I
had chosen Henryson rather than Dunbar.

This development has not yet reached the height it is now
likely to attain. The teaching of Scottish literature is still
badly handicapped by the lack of textbooks at a cost students
can afford. Considering the present costs of book production
this is not likely to be rectified in the immediate future.
Nevertheless the position is very much better than it was
forty or fifty years ago. Excellent work on Henryson is to be
found in many books published in recent years.

In the Introduction to his *Penguin Book of Scottish Verse*

(1970), Dr Tom Scott gives Henryson pride of place over
Dunbar, but on, I think, questionable grounds. He observes
that the difference between Henryson and Dunbar is

seen in the very forms they use, the European traditions they draw
upon. Henrysoun was a natural story-teller, he saw life as a con-
tinuous and integrated whole in which every part had its place –
whether in that proper place or not. Dunbar is essentially a lyric
poet, a poet of mood and variety, his vision more fragmentary,
'now sound, now seik, now dansand merry, now like to dee', and
his forms are song-forms rather than narrative ones. His range of
lyric form, and of mood and emotion, is immense, and in this he
has no rival in his century, and few in any century. He is supremely
the makar; the fashioner of an artefact rather than the conveyor of
a philosophy, a vision, new ideas or values, or any other kind of
utterance. For of these two chief ingredients of poetry, utterance
and artefact, most poets tend more to one than the other, though
all poets must have something of both to be poets at all in more than
the courtesy sense. And Dunbar has intensity of utterance, passion,
in many of his poems: but – and this is something new in Scottish
poetry at this time – it is most intense when most self-centred.
Other poets, Barbour, Hary, Henrysoun, for example, are con-
cerned not about themselves but about the nation, or humanity, or
something far beyond mere individuality: they are invisible in their
own poems. But Dunbar's chief concern, and I cannot but see in
this a spiritual inferiority to Henrysoun, is Dunbar. He is most
lyrical when he is most self-concerned, as in *The Petition of the
Gray Horse, Auld Dunbar*. Here, indeed , we may discern a 'modern'
as distinct from a medieval or classical trait, for he is the first Scots
poet of stature to manifest the personalism which has led poetry to
its present nadir; the great art which once was the highest of public
virtues becomes a petty private vice. Homer sang of Achilles,
Virgil of Aeneas, Dante of Beatrice, Shakespeare of a host of heroes
and anti-heroes, Barbour of Bruce, Hary of Wallace, but Dunbar
sings mostly of Dunbar, and when a poet has no better subject for
his work than himself, there is no reason why other people should
care tuppence, and the art declines in social value to mere dood-
ling.

This won't do. Consider in the light of it Dante's *Divine Comedy* or Byron's *Childe Harold*, Goethe's *Faust* or Wordsworth's *Excursion*. Jacques Barzun* speaks of the 'playwright's vision' of the romantic lyrist: 'He is in effect a dramatist using his own self as a sensitive plate to catch whatever molecular or spiritual motion the outer world may supply.' 'For,' as Robert Langbaum says in *The Poetry of Experience* (London, 1957),

the poetry of experience is, in its meaning if not its events, autobiographical both for the writer and the reader. The observer is thus a character, not in the Aristotelian sense of a moral force to be judged morally, but in the modern sense of a pole for sympathy – the means by which writer and reader project themselves into the poem, the one to communicate, the other to apprehend it as an experience.

W. H. Auden in *The Enchafèd Flood* (New York, 1950) quotes Baudelaire asking: 'What is the modern conception of art? To create a suggestive magic including at the same time object and subject, the world outside the artist, and the artist himself.' Dr Scott should remember Fritz Kaufmann, who in his *Sprache als Schöpfung* contends that in the modern world all the ostensible themes and subjects of the poet will tend to be in the first place simply allegories for the creative process itself. Or, as Cecil Day Lewis says, 'the poetic myths are dead; and the poetic image, which is the myth of the individual, reigns in their stead'.

Dr M. M. Gray was right in saying:

Dunbar, more often than Henryson, has been claimed as the greatest Scottish poet before Burns, but Dunbar never proved his supremacy by handling a subject that tested his powers to the uttermost. Almost all his poems are occasional, they show facets of his poetic genius, no one poem shows all the fine qualities of his

* *Romanticism and the Modern Ego*, London ,1944.

art. Dunbar's world was too much for him; the thwarted ambition and sense of injustice are too continuously reflected in his poetry . . . We are left with the impression that he was capable of greater things than he actually achieved, save in prosody.

It was long the way of writers on Scottish poetry to call Henryson a Chaucerian and to imply that his work was derivative and that he was really a mere imitator of Chaucer. Dr Kurt Wittig, in his *The Scottish Tradition in Literature* (Edinburgh and London, 1958), expresses the view held by all competent scholars today when he says:

It has hitherto been customary to call Henryson, together with James I, Dunbar, and Gavin Douglas a 'Scottish Chaucerian'. True, they introduced into Scots literature Chaucer's example and his handling of themes derived from European literature, and recognized him as their master. But they are far from imitating Chaucer in the same way as Lydgate and Occleve; they have so much besides Chaucerian matter that I prefer to call them by their Scots name of 'makars'. James I alone – if he was the author of the *Kingis Quair* – is a real imitator of Chaucer, but even he shows more originality in doing so than Chaucer's English disciples. Instead of a dream allegory the poet presents us with a real event, his own personal love, with a wealth of perception and an eye alert to the fleeting impressions of fire, reflexions, colour, running water, jumping fish. There is moral seriousness of purpose in his glorification of matrimonial instead of courtly love, and in his essentially Christian outlook. Not unlike Barbour the poet stresses the autonomy of the will, even against Fortune . . . All these traits have their special weight in the Scottish tradition. Robert Henryson's debt to Chaucer is great, and he is the first to acknowledge it. But he does not imitate. He assimilates Chaucer's conception of poetry and creates from this artistic centre. In a more limited field he achieves (as Tillyard observes) the same artistic level as his master, and there are even passages where Henryson surpasses Chaucer, as in the introduction to the *Testament*, or the meeting of the lovers. He fertilizes Chaucer's heritage with his own native tradition and achieves a new subtlety which is totally his own.

Dr Agnes Mure Mackenzie put the matter very well when she wrote:

Of the major poets of his century, Henryson is, superficially, most like Chaucer in temper and outlook and in the peculiar quality of his humour. The likeness, however – the more as it extends to choice of subject – throws strongly into relief his very marked individuality both as man and as poet, which shows most clearly in, precisely, the poem whose subject is avowedly suggested by Chaucer. Chaucer's *Troylus and Criseyde* had been a version of a favourite medieval addition to the tale of Troy ... Shakespeare was to take it up again, with its passion and pity turned to a sardonic anger of disillusionment. Henryson set himself to continue Chaucer's poem, in a spirit that is neither Chaucer's nor Shakespeare's; it is nearer, in fact, the temper of Shakespeare's own tragedies. Instead of the novelist's analysis of emotion in Chaucer's *Troylus*, which is in fact the first great English novel, there is a fierce condensation, a darker and sterner pity, not pathos but the swordstroke tragedy of the ballads ... The whole thing has a stark sense of the east wind – one of those bleak Fife days with white water on the Firth. But its stern justice has a profound and aching pity, and something also of the sense of redemption that comes at the close of a tragedy of Shakespeare's. It is not by any means Henryson's only note. He can write things of the shrewdest and liveliest humour, with a homely realism instead of the stately pageant of the gods; but even under their most whimsical there is always a sense of the tragic littleness of humanity, and below that again, what is not common anywhere in that century, a grave underlying assurance of stable law.*

Little is known of Henryson's life. His dates are usually accepted as c. 1420–c. 1490. If for various reasons he has commended himself less quickly to contemporary Scottish poets and others, the headway gained by Dunbar seems to be rapidly reduced in the past year or two.

There is now a consensus of judgement that regards Henryson as the greatest of our great makars. Literary his-

* Vide her *Scottish Literature to 1714*, London, 1933.

torians and other commentators in the bad period of the century preceding the twenties of our own century were wont to group together as the great five Henryson, Dunbar, Douglas, Lyndsay, and King James I; but in the critical atmosphere prevailing today it is clear that Henryson (who was, with the exception of King James, the youngest of them) is the greatest. Our Gaelic poets and our Latin poets are not under consideration in this context.

In *Studies on Scottish Literature* (Vol. VIII, No. 1, July 1970), Professor Florence H. Ridley publishes 'A check list, 1956–1968 for study of *The Kingis Quair*, the poetry of Robert Henryson, Gavin Douglas, and William Dunbar'. She says:

Much of this poetry has been known since the early sixteenth century; yet only within the past fifty years has it begun to receive competent study and to be made the subject of truly perceptive criticism. In the four centuries immediately following their emergence, some sixty articles dealing with James I (as author of *The Kingis Quair*), Henryson, Douglas and Dunbar appeared. In the last twelve years one hundred and four such articles have appeared, two volumes of selections from Douglas's poetry, one each from that of Henryson and Dunbar, and new editions of the collected works of the latter two poets. We are it would seem in the midst of a Middle Scots boom! And yet there is still no satisfactory book-length treatment of the Middle Scots poets as a group or of any one of them as an individual. The major poems of Henryson and Dunbar have never received adequate critical study, that on the poems of Douglas is minimal, and the problems of authorship, period, even meaning of *The Kingis Quair* remain to be solved. Thus although in the last twelve years much has been accomplished in study of these poets, largely through the efforts of such men as Robert Kinsley, Denton Fox, D. F. C. Coldwell, and John MacQueen, much remains to be done.

In addition to volumes of selections, anthologies and new editions of the *œuvres* of particular poets, Professor Ridley lists no fewer than thirty published literary-critical essays on

Henryson as against about ten devoted to Dunbar, and it is a pointer to the extension of Scottish Studies in Canada and the United States that unpublished dissertations include S. J. Harth: *Convention and Creation in the Poetry of Robert Henryson* (University of Chicago, 1960) and J. W. Proctor's *A Description of the Fifteenth Century Scots Dialect of Robert Henryson based on a Complete Concordance of his Works* (University of Missouri, 1966).

Mr Maurice Lindsay in his Introduction to the latest edition of *A Book of Scottish Verse* in the World's Classics Series (1967) puts the matter in a nutshell when he says: 'He infuses all his poetry with his own warm and kindly personality. This schoolmaster of Dunfermline must have been a good person to know.'

I am happy to think that in this fully representative, yet very cheap, selection a great new public may accrue to Henryson and agree with Mr Lindsay and all the others I name in finding him a real and very welcome discovery.

HUGH MACDIARMID

Further Recommended Reading

John MacQueen, *Robert Henryson. A Study of the Major Narrative Poems*, London, 1967.

M. Y. Stearns, *Robert Henryson*, New York, 1949.

E. M. W. Tillyard, in *Five Poems 1470–1870*, London, 1948, pp. 5–29.

A. C. Spearing, in *Criticism and Medieval Poetry*, London, 1964, pp. 118–44.

Edwin Muir, in *Literature and Society*, London, 1949, pp. 7–19.

The Testament of Cresseid

Ane doolie sessoun to ane cairfull dyte
Suld correspond, and be equivalent.
Richt sa it wes quhen I began to wryte
This tragedie, the wedder richt fervent,
Quhen Aries, in middis of the Lent,
Schouris of haill can fra the north discend,
That scantlie fra the cauld I micht defend.

Yit nevertheles within myne oratur
I stude, quhen Titan had his bemis bricht
Withdrawin doun, and sylit under cure
And fair Venus, the bewtie of the nicht,
Uprais, and set unto the west full richt
Hir goldin face in oppositioun
Of God Phebus direct discending doun.

Throw out the glas hir bemis brast sa fair
That I micht se on everie syde me by
The Northin wind had purifyit the Air
And sched the mistie cloudis fra the sky,
The froist freisit, the blastis bitterly
Fra Pole Artick come quhisling loud and schill,
And causit me remufe aganis my will.

doolie mournful
dyte writing, poem
cauld cold
oratur oratory

sylit hidden
cure cover
brast burst, pierced

For I traistit that Venus, luifis Quene,
To quhome sum tyme I hecht obedience,
My faidit hart of lufe scho wald mak grene,
And therupon with humbill reverence,
I thocht to pray hir hie Magnificence;
Bot for greit cald as than I lattit was,
And in my Chalmer to the fyre can pas.

Thocht lufe be hait, yit in ane man of age
It kendillis nocht sa sone as in youtheid,
Of quhome the blude is flowing in ane rage,
And in the auld the curage doif and deid,
Of quhilk the fyre outward is best remeid;
To help be Phisike quhair that nature faillit
I am expert, for baith I have assailit.

I mend the fyre and beikit me about,
Than tuik ane drink my spreitis to comfort,
And armit me weill fra the cauld thairout:
To cut the winter nicht and mak it schort,
I tuik ane Quair, and left all uther sport,
Writtin be worthie Chaucer glorious,
Of fair Creisseid, and worthie Troylus.

And thair I fand, efter that Diomeid
Ressavit had that Lady bricht of hew,
How Troilus neir out of wit abraid,
And weipit soir with visage paill of hew;
For quhilk wanhope his teiris can renew

luifis love's	*doif* dull
sum tyme formerly	*remeid* remedy
hecht promised	*assailit* tried
lattit hindered, frustrated	*beikit* warmed
Chalmer room	*Quair* book
hait hot	*abraid* started
kendillis kindles	*wanhope* despair
sone soon	

Quhill Esperus rejoisit him agane,
Thus quhyle in Joy he levit, quhyle in pane.

Of hir behest he had greit comforting,
Traisting to Troy that scho suld mak retour,
Quhilk he desyrit maist of eirdly thing
Forquhy scho was his only Paramour;
Bot quhen he saw passit baith day and hour
Of hir ganecome, than sorrow can oppres
His wofull hart in cair and hevines.

Of his distres me neidis nocht reheirs,
For worthie Chauceir in the samin buik
In gudelie termis and in Joly veirs
Compylit hes his cairis, quha will luik.
To brek my sleip ane uther quair I tuik,
In quhilk I fand the fatall destenie
Of fair Cresseid, that endit wretchitlie.

Quha wait gif all that Chauceir wrait was trew?
Nor I wait nocht gif this narratioun
Be authoreist, or fenyeit of the new
Be sum Poeit, throw his Inventioun,
Maid to report the Lamentatioun
And wofull end of this lustie Creisseid,
And quhat distres scho thoillit, and quhat deid.

Quhen Diomeid had all his appetyte,
And mair, fulfillit of this fair Ladie,
Upon ane uther he set his haill delyte
And send to hir ane Lybell of repudie,
And hir excludit fra his companie.

quhill till	*wait* knows
quhyle sometimes	*fenyeit* newly invented
forquhy because	*thoillit* suffered
ganecome return	

Than desolait scho walkit up and doun,
And sum men sayis into the Court commoun.

O fair Creisseid, the flour and A per se
Of Troy and Grece, how was thou fortunait!
To change in filth all thy Feminitie,
And be with fleschlie lust sa maculait,
And go amang the Greikis air and lait
Sa giglotlike, takand thy foull plesance!
I have pietie thou suld fall sic mischance.

Yit nevertheless quhat ever men deme or say
In scornefull langage of thy brukkilnes,
I sall excuse, als far furth as I may,
Thy womanheid, thy wisdome and fairnes:
The quhilk Fortoun hes put to sic distres
As hir pleisit, and nathing throw the gilt
Of the, throw wickit langage to be spilt.

This fair Lady, in this wyse destitute
Of all comfort and consolatioun,
Richt privelie, but fellowscip, on fute
Disagysit passit far out of the toun
Ane myle or twa, unto ane Mansioun
Beildit full gay, quhair hir father Calchas
Quhilk than amang the Greikis dwelland was.

fortunait ordained   *brukkilnes* frailty
maculait stained   *but* without
air early   *disagysit* disguised
giglotlike wantonly   *beildit* built for shelter
deme denounce

Quhen he hir saw, the caus he can Inquyre
Of hir cumming; scho said, siching full soir:
'Fra Diomeid had gottin his desyre
He wox werie, and wald of me no moir.'
Quod Calchas, 'douchter, weip thou not thairfoir;
Peraventure all cummis for the best;
Welcum to me, thou art full deir ane Gest.'

This auld Calchas, efter the Law was tho,
Wes keiper of the Tempill as ane Preist,
In quhilk Venus and hir Sone Cupido
War honourit, and his Chalmer was thame neist,
To quhilk Cresseid with baill aneuch in breist
Usit to pas, hir prayeris for to say.
Quhill at the last, upon ane Solempne day,

As custome was, the pepill far and neir
Befoir the none, unto the Tempill went,
With Sacrifice, devoit in thair maneir:
Bot still Cresseid, hevie in hir Intent,
Into the Kirk wald not hir self present,
For giving of the pepill ony deming
Of hir expuls fra Diomeid the King:

Bot past into ane secreit Orature
Quhair scho micht weip hir wofull desteny,
Behind hir bak scho cloisit fast the dure
And on hir kneis bair fell doun in hy.
Upon Venus and Cupide angerly
Scho cryit out, and said on this same wyse,
'Allace that ever I maid you Sacrifice.

siching sighing
fra after
Gest guest
tho then
neist next

baill aneuch trouble enough
devoit devout
for giving lest she should give
hy haste

'Ye give me anis ane devine responsaill
That I suld be the flour of luif in Troy,
Now am I maid ane unworthie outwaill,
And all in cair translatit is my Joy,
Quha sall me gyde? quha sall me now convoy
Sen I fra Diomeid and Nobill Troylus
Am clene excludit, as abject odious?

'O fals Cupide, is nane to wyte bot thow,
And thy Mother, of lufe the blind Goddes!
Ye causit me alwayis understand and trow
The seid of lufe was sawin in my face,
And ay grew grene throw your supplie and grace.
Bot now allace that seid with froist is slane,
And I fra luifferis left and all forlane.'

Quhen this was said, doun in ane extasie,
Ravischit in spreit, intill ane dreame scho fell,
And be apperance hard, quhair scho did ly,
Cupide the King ringand ane silver bell,
Quhilk men micht heir fra hevin unto hell;
At quhais sound befoir Cupide appeiris
The seven Planetis discending fra thair Spheiris,

Quhilk hes power of all thing generabill
To reull and steir be thair greit Influence,
Wedder and wind, and coursis variabill:
And first of all Saturne gave his sentence,
Quhilk gave to Cupide litill reverence,
Bot, as ane busteous Churle on his maneir,
Come crabitlie with auster luik and cheir.

---

responsaill answer to prayer   *wyte* blame
outwaill outcast   *supplie* support
abject cast-off   *busteous* blustering

His face [fronsit], his lyre was lyke the Leid,
His teith chatterit, and cheverit with the Chin,
His Ene drowpit, how sonkin in his heid,
Out of his Nois and Meldrop fast can rin,
With lippis bla and cheikis leine and thin;
The Iceschoklis that fra his hair doun hang
Was wonder greit, and as ane speir als lang.

Atouir his belt his lyart lokkis lay
Felterit unfair, ouirfret with Froistis hoir,
His garmound and his gyis full gay of gray,
His widderit weid fra him the wind out woir;
Ane busteous bow within his hand he boir,
Under his girdill ane flasche of felloun flanis,
Fedderit with Ice, and heidit with hailstanis.

Than Juppiter, richt fair and amiabill,
God of the Starnis in the Firmament,
And Nureis to all thing generabill,
Fra his Father Saturne far different,
With burelie face, and browis bricht and brent,
Upon his heid ane Garland, wonder gay,
Of flouris fair, as it had bene in May.

fronsit wrinkled   *Felterit* matted
lyre complexion   *ouirfret* laced over
cheverit shivered   *gyis* attire
how hollow   *weid* clothing
Nois nose   *flasche* sheaf
Meldrop mucus drop   *felloun* cruel
bla livid   *flanis* arrows
Iceschoklis icicles   *burelie* goodly
atouir about   *brent* smooth
lyart hoary

His voice was cleir, as Cristall wer his Ene,
As goldin wyre sa glitterand was his hair;
His garmound and his gyis full [gay] of grene,
With golden listis gilt on everie gair;
Ane burelie brand about his midill bair;
In his richt hand he had ane groundin speir,
Of his Father the wraith fra us to weir.

Nixt efter him come Mars, the God of Ire,
Of strife, debait, and all dissensioun,
To chide and fecht, als feirs as ony fyre;
In hard Harnes, hewmound and Habirgeoun,
And on his hanche ane roustie fell Fachioun;
And in his hand he had ane roustie sword;
Wrything his face with mony angrie word,

Schaikand his sword, befoir Cupide he come
With reid visage, and grislie glowrand Ene;
And at his mouth ane bullar stude of fome
Lyke to ane Bair quhetting his Tuskis kene,
Richt Tui[t]lyeour lyke, but temperance in tene;
Ane horne he blew, with mony bosteous brag,
Quhilk all this warld with weir hes maid to wag.

Than fair Phebus, Lanterne & Lamp of licht
Of man and beist, baith frute and flourisching,
Tender Nureis, and banischer of nicht,
And of the warld causing, be his moving
And Influence, lyfe in all eirdlie thing,

listis edges	*glowrand* glaring
gair strip	*bullar* mass of bubbles
groundin sharpened	*Bair* boar
weir ward	*Tui[t]lyeour lyke* brawler-like,
hewmound helmet	quarrelsome
Habirgeoun mail coat	*tene* anger
roustie rusty	*bosteous* rough
Fachioun short sword	*weir* war

Without comfort of quhome, of force to nocht
Must all ga die that in this warld is wrocht.

As King Royall he raid upon his Chair
The quhilk Phaeton gydit sym tyme upricht;
The brichtnes of his face quhen it was bair
Nane micht behald for peirsing of his sicht.
This goldin Cart with fyrie bemis bricht
Four yokkit steidis full different of hew,
But bait or tyring, throw the Spheiris drew.

The first was soyr, with Mane als reid as Rois,
Callit Eoye into the Orient;
The secund steid to Name hecht Ethios,
Quhitlie and paill, and sum deill ascendent;
The thrid Peros, richt hait and richt fervent;
The feird was blak, callit Philologie
Quhilk rollis Phebus doun into the sey.

Venus was thair present that goddes gay,
Hir Sonnis querrell for to defend and mak
Hir awin complaint, cled in ane nyce array,
The ane half grene, the uther half Sabill black;
Quhyte hair as gold kemmit and sched abak;
Bot in hir face semit greit variance,
Quhyles perfyte treuth, and quhyles Inconstance

Under smyling scho was dissimulait,
Provocative, with blenkis Amorous,
And suddanely changit and alterait,
Angrie as ony Serpent vennemous
Richt pungitive, with wordis odious.

but bait without pause
soyr sorrel
Eoye Eoüs, belonging to the
   dawn

hecht called
sum deill somewhat
blenkis glances
pungitive pungent

Thus variant scho was, quha list tak keip,
With ane Eye lauch, and with the uther weip.

In taikning that all fleschelie Paramour
Quhilk Venus hes in reull and governance,
Is sum tyme sweit, sum tyme bitter and sour
Richt unstabill, and full of variance,
Mingit with cairfull Joy and fals plesance,
Now hait, now cauld, now blyith, now full of wo,
Now grene as leif, now widderit and ago.

With buik in hand than come Mercurius,
Richt Eloquent, and full of Rethorie,
With polite termis and delicious,
With pen and Ink to report al reddie,
Setting sangis and singand merilie:
His Hude was reid, heklit atouir his Croun,
Lyke to ane Poeit of the auld fassoun.

Boxis he bair with fine Electuairis,
And sugerit Syropis for digestioun,
Spycis belangand to the Pothecairis,
With mony hailsum sweit Confectioun,
Doctour in Phisick cled in ane Skarlot goun,
And furrit weill, as sic ane aucht to be,
Honest and gude, and not ane word culd le.

Nixt efter him come Lady Cynthia,
The last of all, and swiftest in hir Spheir,
Of colour blak, buskit with hornis twa,
And in the nicht scho listis best appeir.
Haw as the Leid, of colour nathing cleir;

keip heed	*fassoun* fashion
taikning tokening	*buskit* adorned
mingit mingled	*haw* wan
ago gone	

For all hir licht scho borrowis at hir brother
Titan, for of hir self scho hes nane uther.

Hir gyse was gray, and ful of spottis blak,
And on hir breist ane Churle paintit full evin,
Beirand ane bunche of Thornis on his bak,
Quhilk for his thift micht clim na nar the hevin.
Thus quhen thay gadderit war, thir Goddes sevin,
Mercurius thay cheisit with ane assent
To be foirspeikar in the Parliament.

Quha had bene thair, and liken for to heir
His facound toung, and termis exquisite,
Of Rethorick the prettick he micht leir,
In breif Sermone ane pregnant sentence wryte:
Befoir Cupide veiling his Cap alyte,
Speiris the caus of that vocatioun,
And he anone schew his Intentioun.

'Lo!' (quod Cupide), 'quha will blaspheme the name
Of his awin God, outher in word or deid,
To all Goddis he dois baith lak and schame,
And suld have bitter panis to his meid.
I say this by yone wretchit Cresseid,
The quilk throw me was sum tyme flour of lufe,
Me and my Mother starklie can reprufe.

nar nearer   *alyte* a little
cheisit chose   *speiris* asks
facound eloquent   *schew* show
prettick practice   *lak* reproach
leir learn

'Saying of hir greit Infelicitie
I was the caus, and my Mother Venus,
Ane blind Goddes, hir cald, that micht not se,
With sclander and defame Injurious;
Thus hir leving unclene and Lecherous
Scho wald returne on me and my Mother,
To quhome I schew my grace abone all uther.

'And sen ye ar all sevin deificait,
Participant of devyne sapience,
This greit Injurie done to our hie estait
Me think with pane we suld mak recompence;
Was never to Goddes done sic violence.
Asweill for yow, as for myself I say,
Thairfoir ga help to revenge I yow pray.'

Mercurius to Cupide gave answeir
And said: 'Schir King my counsall is that ye
Refer yow to the hiest planeit heir,
And tak to him the lawest of degre,
The pane of Cresseid for to modifie;
As god Saturne, with him tak Cynthia.'
'I am content' (quod he), 'to tak thay twa.'

Than thus proceidit Saturne and the Mone,
Quhen thay the mater rypelie had degest,
For the dispyte to Cupide scho had done,
And to Venus oppin and manifest,
In all hir lyfe with pane to be opprest,
And torment sair, with seiknes Incurabill,
And to all lovers be abhominabill.

sen since   *modifie* determine

This duleful sentence Saturne tuik on hand,
And passit doun quhair cairfull Cresseid lay,
And on hir heid he laid ane frostie wand;
Than lawfullie on this wyse can he say:
'Thy greit fairnes and all thy bewtie gay,
Thy wantoun blude, and eik thy goldin Hair,
Heir I exclude fra the for evermair.

'I change thy mirth into Melancholy,
Quhilk is the Mother of all pensivenes;
Thy Moisture and thy heit in cald and dry;
Thyne Insolence, thy play and wantones
To greit diseis; thy Pomp and thy riches
In mortall neid; and greit penuritie
Thou suffer sall, and as ane beggar die.'

O cruell Saturne! fraward and angrie,
Hard is thy dome, and to malitious;
On fair Cresseid quhy hes thou na mercie,
Quhilk was sa sweit, gentill and amorous?
Withdraw thy sentence and be gracious
As thou was never; so schawis thow thy deid,
Ane wraikfull sentence gevin on fair Cresseid.

Than Cynthia, quhen Saturne past away,
Out of hir sait discendit doun belyve,
And red ane bill on Cresseid quhair scho lay,
Contening this sentence diffinityve:
'Fra heit of bodie I the now depryve,
And to thy seiknes sal be na recure,
Bot in dolour thy dayis to Indure.

lawfullie in accordance with the   *wraikfull* revengeful
   judgement   *belyve* quickly

'Thy Cristall Ene minglit with blude I mak,
Thy voice sa cleir, unplesand hoir and hace,
Thy lustie lyre ouirspred with spottis blak,
And lumpis haw appeirand in thy face.
Quhair thou cumis, Ilk man sal fle the place.
This sall thou go begging fra hous to hous
With Cop and Clapper lyke ane Lazarous.'

This doolie dreame, this uglye visioun
Brocht to ane end, Cresseid fra it awoik,
And all that Court and convocatioun
Vanischit away, than rais scho up and tuik
Ane poleist glas, and hir schaddow culd luik:
And quhen scho saw hir face sa deformait
Gif scho in hart was wa aneuch God wait.

Weiping full sair, 'Lo quhat it is' (quod sche),
'With fraward langage for to mufe and steir
Our craibit Goddis, and sa is sene on me!
My blaspheming now have I bocht full deir.
All eirdlie Joy and mirth I set areir.
Allace this day, allace this wofull tyde,
Quhen I began with my Goddis for to Chyde.'

Be this was said ane Chyld come fra the Hall
To warne Cresseid the Supper was reddy,
First knokkit at the dure, and syne culd call:
'Madame your Father biddis yow cum in hy.
He hes mervell sa lang on grouf ye ly,
And sayis your prayers bene to lang sum deill:
The goddis wait all your Intent full weill.'

hoir old (hoar)	*wait* knows
hace harsh	*areir* behind
lyre skin	*hy* haste
Lazarous leper	*grouf* grovelling
wa aneuch woeful enough	

Quod scho: 'Fair Chyld ga to my Father deir,
And pray him cum to speik with me anone.'
And sa he did, and said: 'douchter quhat cheir?'
'Allace' (quod scho), 'Father my mirth is gone.'
'How sa' (quod he); and scho can all expone
As I have tauld, the vengeance and the wraik
For hir trespas, Cupide on hir culd tak.

He luikit on hir uglye Lipper face,
The quhilk befor was quhyte as Lillie flour,
Wringand his handis oftymes he said allace
That he had levit to se that wofull hour,
For he knew weill that thair was na succour
To hir seiknes, and that dowblit his pane.
Thus was thair cair aneuch betuix thame twane.

Quhen thay togidder murnit had full lang,
Quod Cresseid: 'Father, I wald not be kend.
Thairfoir in secreit wyse ye let me gang
Into yone Hospitall at the tounis end.
And thidder sum meit for Cheritie me send
To leif upon, for all mirth in this eird
Is fra me gane, sic is my wickit weird.'

Than in ane Mantill and ane bawer Hat,
With Cop and Clapper wonder prively,
He opnit ane secreit yet, and out thair at
Convoyit hir, that na man suld espy,
Into ane Village half ane myle thairby,
Delyverit hir in at the Spittaill hous,
And daylie sent hir part of his Almous.

wraik punishment   *bawer* beaver
kend known   *yet* gate
eird earth   *Spittaill hous* hospital
weird fate   *Almous* alms

Sum knew her weill, & sum had na knawledge
Of hir becaus scho was sa deformait,
With bylis blak ouirspred in hir visage,
And hir fair colour faidit and alterait.
Yit thay presumit for her hie regrait
And still murning, scho was of Nobill kin:
With better will thairfoir they tuik hir in.

The day passit, and Phebus went to rest,
The Cloudis blak ouirquhelmit all the sky.
God wait gif Cresseid was ane sorrowfull Gest,
Seing that uncouth fair and Harbery:
But meit or drink scho dressit hir to ly
In ane dark Corner of the Hous allone.
And on this wyse weiping, scho maid her mone:

The Complaint of Cresseid

'O sop of sorrow, sonkin into cair:
O Cative Creisseid, for now and ever mair,
Gane is thy Joy and all thy mirth in Eird,
Of all blyithnes now art thou blaiknit bair.
Thair is na Salve may saif the of thy sair,
Fell is thy Fortoun, wickit is thy weird:
Thy blys is baneist, and thy baill on breird,
Under the Eirth, God gif I gravin wer:
Quhair nane of Grece nor yit of Troy micht heird.

bylis boils   *Cative* wretched
regrait grief   *blaiknit* blackened
Harbery lodging   *baill on breird* woe burgeoning
sonkin sunken

'Quhair is thy Chalmer wantounlie besene?
With burely bed and bankouris browderit bene,
Spycis and Wyne to thy Collatioun,
The Cowpis all of gold and silver schene:
The sweit Meitis, servit on plaittis clene,
With Saipheron sals of ane gud sessoun:
Thy gay garmentis with mony gudely Goun,
Thy plesand Lawn pinnit with goldin prene:
All is areir, thy greit Royall Renoun.

'Quhair is thy garding with thir greissis gay?
And fresche flowris, quhilk the Quene Floray:
Had paintit plesandly in everie pane,
Quhair thou was wont full merilye in May,
To walk and tak the dew be it was day
And heir the Merle and Mawis mony ane,
With Ladyis fair in Carrolling to gane,
And se the Royall Rinkis in thair array,
In garmentis gay garnischit on everie grane.

'Thy greit triumphand fame and hie honour,
Quhair thou was callit of Eirdlye wichtis Flour,
All is decayit, thy weird is welterit so.
Thy hie estait is turnit in darknes dour.
This Lipper Ludge tak for thy burelie Bour.
And for thy Bed tak now ane bunche of stro,
For waillit Wyne, and Meitis thou had tho,

wantounlie gaily
besene furnished
burely pleasant
bankouris tapestries
browderit embroidered
bene well
Saipheron saffron
sals sauce
sessoun seasoning
prene pin

pane flower bed
Carrolling circular dances with
    song
Rinkis personages
grane colour
welterit turned
dour enduring
Ludge lodging
waillit choice
tho then

Tak mowlit Breid, Peirrie and Ceder sour:
Bot Cop and Clapper, now is all ago.

'My cleir voice, and courtlie carrolling,
Quhair I was wont with Ladyis for to sing,
Is rawk as Ruik, full hiddeous hoir and hace,
My plesand port all utheris precelling:
Of lustines I was hald maist conding.
Now is deformit the Figour of my face,
To luik on it, na Leid now lyking hes:
Sowpit in syte, I say with sair siching,
Ludgeit amang the Lipper Leid allace.

'O Ladyis fair of Troy and Grece, attend
My miserie, quhilk nane may comprehend.
My frivoll Fortoun, my Infelicitie:
My greit mischeif quhilk na man can amend.
Be war in tyme, approchis neir the end,
And in your mynd ane mirrour mak of me:
As I am now, peradventure that ye
For all your micht may cum to that same end,
Or ellis war, gif ony war may be.

'Nocht is your fairnes bot ane faiding flour,
Nocht is your famous laud and hie honour
Bot wind Inflat in uther mennis eiris.
Your roising reid to rotting sall retour:
Exempill mak of me in your Memour,
Quhilk of sic thingis wofull witnes beiris,
All Welth in Eird, away as Wind it weiris.
Be war thairfoir, approchis neir the hour:
Fortoun is fikkill, quhen scho beginnis & steiris.'

mowlit mouldy	*conding* worthy
Peirrie perry	*war* worse
Ceder cider	*roising* rose
rawk hoarse	*steiris* stirs
precelling excelling	

Thus chydand with hir drerie destenye,
Weiping, scho woik the nicht fra end to end.
Bot all in vane; hir dule, hir cairfull cry
Micht not remeid, nor yit hir murning mend.
Ane Lipper Lady rais and till hir wend,
And said: 'quhy spurnis thow aganis the Wall,
To sla thy self, and mend nathing at all?

'Sen thy weiping dowbillis bot thy wo,
I counsall the mak vertew of ane neid.
To leir to clap thy Clapper to and fro,
And leir efter the Law of Lipper Leid.'
Thair was na buit, bot furth with thame scho yeid,
Fra place to place, quhill cauld and hounger sair
Compellit hir to be ane rank beggair.

That samin tyme of Troy the Garnisoun,
Quhilk had to chiftane worthie Troylus,
Throw Jeopardie of Weir had strikken doun
Knichtis of Grece in number mervellous,
With greit tryumphe and Laude victorious
Agane to Troy [richt] Royallie they raid
The way quhair Cresseid with the Lipper baid.

Seing that companie thai come all with ane stevin
Thay gaif ane cry and schuik coppis gude speid.
Said 'worthie Lordis for goddis lufe of Hevin,
To us Lipper part of your Almous deid.'
Than to thair cry Nobill Troylus tuik heid,
Having pietie, neir by the place can pas:
Quhair Cresseid sat, not witting quhat scho was.

dule sorrow   *buit* help
remeid remedy   *yeid* went
wend went   *baid* dwelt
dowbillis doubles   *(ane) stevin* one voice

Than upon him scho kest up baith hir Ene,
And with ane blenk it come into his thocht,
That he sumtime hir face befoir had sene.
Bot scho was in sic plye he knew hir nocht,
Yit than hir luik into his mynd it brocht
The sweit visage and amorous blenking
Of fair Cresseid sumtyme his awin darling.

Na wonder was, suppois in mynd that he
Tuik hir figure sa sone, and lo now quhy?
The Idole of ane thing, in cace may be
So deip Imprentit in the fantasy
That it deludis the wittis outwardly,
And sa appeiris in forme and lyke estait,
Within the mynd as it was figurait.

Ane spark of lufe than till his hart culd spring
And kendlit all his bodie in ane fyre.
With hait Fewir ane sweit and trimbling
Him tuik, quhill he was reddie to expyre.
To beir his Scheild, his Breist began to tyre
Within ane quhyle he changit mony hew,
And nevertheless not ane ane uther knew.

For Knichtlie pietie and memoriall
Of fair Cresseid, ane Gyrdill can he tak,
Ane Purs of gold, and mony gay Jowall,
And in the Skirt of Cresseid doun can swak;
Than raid away, and not ane word [he] spak,
Pensive in hart, quhill he come to the Toun,
And for greit care oft syis almaist fell doun.

blenk glance   *tuik hir figure* had a mental
plye plight   picture of her
suppois that, although   *swak* flung
                         oft syis often

The lipper folk to Cresseid than can draw,
To se the equall distributioun
Of the Almous, bot quhen the gold thay saw,
Ilk ane to uther prevelie can roun,
And said: 'Yone Lord hes mair affectioun,
How ever it be, unto yone Lazarous
Than to us all, we knaw be his Almous.'

'Quhat Lord is yone' (quod scho), 'have ye na feill,
Hes done to us so greit humanitie?'
'Yes' (quod a Lipper man), 'I knaw him weill,
Schir Troylus it is, gentill and fre:'
Quhen Cresseid understude that it was he,
Stiffer than steill, thair stert ane bitter stound
Throwout hir hart, and fell doun to the ground.

Quhen scho ouircome, with siching sair & sad,
With mony cairfull cry and cald ochane:
'Now is my breist with stormie stoundis stad,
Wrappit in wo, ane wretch full will of wane.'
Than swounit scho oft or scho culd refrane,
And ever in hir swouning cryit scho thus:
'O fals Cresseid and trew Knicht Troylus.

'Thy lufe, thy lawtie, and thy gentilnes,
I countit small in my prosperitie,
Sa elevait I was in wantones,
And clam upon the fickill quheill sa hie:
All Faith and Lufe I promissit to the,
Was in the self fickill and frivolous:
O fals Cresseid, and trew Knicht Troilus.

roun whisper	*full will of wane* uncertain of
feill knowledge	purpose
stound pang	*lawtie* loyalty
stad bestead	*quheill* wheel (of fortune)
	the self myself

'For lufe, of me thou keipt gude continence,
Honest and chaist in conversatioun.
Of all wemen protectour and defence
Thou was, and helpit thair opinioun.
My mynd in fleschelie foull affectioun
Was Inclynit to Lustis Lecherous:
Fy fals Cresseid, O trew Knicht Troylus.

'Lovers be war and tak gude heid about
Quhome that ye lufe, for quhome ye suffer paine.
I lat yow wit, thair is richt few thairout
Quhome ye may traist to have trew lufe agane.
Preif quhen ye will, your labour is in vaine.
Thairfoir, I reid, ye tak thame as ye find,
For thay ar sad as Widdercock in Wind,

'Becaus I knaw the greit unstabilnes
Brukkill as glas, into my self I say,
Traisting in uther als greit unfaithfulnes:
Als unconstant, and als untrew of fay.
Thocht sum be trew, I wait richt few ar thay,
Quha findis treuth lat him his Lady ruse:
Nane but my self as now I will accuse.'

Quhen this was said, with Paper scho sat doun,
And on this maneir maid hir Testament.
'Heir I beteiche my Corps and Carioun
With Wormis and with Taidis to be rent.
My Cop and Clapper and myne Ornament,
And all my gold the Lipper folk sall have:
Quhen I am deid, to burie me in grave.

opinioun good repute	*brukkill* brittle
thairout existing	*fay* faith
preif test	*ruse* praise
sad sober	*beteiche* bequeath
Widdercock weathercock	*Taidis* toads

'This Royal Ring, set with this Rubie reid,
Quhilk Troylus in drowrie to me send,
To him agane I leif it quhen I am deid,
To mak my cairfull deid unto him kend:
Thus I conclude schortlie and mak ane end,
My Spreit I leif to Diane quhair scho dwellis,
To walk with hir in waist Woddis and Wellis.

'O Diomeid, thou hes baith Broche and Belt,
Quhilk Troylus gave me in takning
Of his trew lufe,' and with that word scho swelt.
And sone ane Lipper man tuik of the Ring,
Syne buryit hir withouttin tarying:
To Troylus furthwith the Ring he bair,
And of Cresseid the deith he can declair.

Quhen he had hard hir greit infirmitie,
Hir Legacie and Lamentatioun,
And how scho endit in sic povertie,
He swelt for wo, and fell doun in ane swoun,
For greit sorrow his hart to brist was boun:
Siching full sadlie, said: 'I can no moir,
Scho was untrew, and wo is me thairfoir.'

Sum said he maid ane Tomb of Merbell gray,
And wrait hir name and superscriptioun,
And laid it on hir grave quhair that scho lay,
In goldin Letteris, conteining this ressoun:
'Lo, fair Ladyis, Crisseid, of Troyis toun,
Sumtyme countit the flour of Womanheid,
Under this stane lait Lipper lyis deid.'

drowrie dowry   *swelt* expired
kend known   *boun* ready
Wellis marshes

Now, worthie Wemen, in this Ballet schort,
Made for your worschip and Instructioun,
Of Cheritie, I monische and exhort,
Ming not your lufe with fals deceptioun.
Beir in your mynd this schort conclusioun
Of fair Cresseid, as I have said befoir.
Sen scho is deid, I speik of hir no moir.

monische admonish   *ming* mingle

The Preiching of the Swallow

The hie prudence, and wirking mervelous,
The profound wit off God omnipotent,
Is sa perfyte, and so Ingenious,
Excellent ffar all mannis Jugement;
For quhy to him all thing is ay present,
Rycht as it is, or ony tyme sall be,
Befoir the sicht off his Divinitie.

Thairfoir our Saull with Sensualitie
So fetterit is in presoun Corporall,
We may not cleirlie understand nor se
God as he is, nor thingis Celestiall:
Our mirk and deidlie corps Naturall
Blindis the Spirituall operatioun,
Lyke as ane man wer bundin in presoun.

In Metaphisik Aristotell sayis
That mannis Saull is lyke ane Bakkis Ee,
Quhilk lurkis still als lang as licht off day is,
And in the gloming cummis furth to fle;
Hir Ene ar waik, the Sone scho may not se:
Sa is our Saull with fantasie opprest,
To knaw the thingis in nature manifest.

For God is in his power Infinite,
And mannis Saull is febill and over small,
Off understanding waik and unperfite,
To comprehend him that contenis all.
Nane suld presume, be ressoun naturall,
To seirche the secreitis off the Trinitie,
Bot trow fermelie, and lat all ressoun be.

excellent excelling   *or* before
for quhy because

Yit nevertheles we may haif knawlegeing
Off God almychtie, be his Creatouris,
That he is gude, ffair, wyis and bening;
Exempill tak be thir Jolie flouris,
Rycht sweit off smell, and plesant off colouris.
Sum grene, sum blew, sum purpour, quhyte, and reid,
Thus distribute be gift off his Godheid.

The firmament payntit with sternis cleir,
From eist to west rolland in cirkill round,
And everilk Planet in his proper Spheir,
In moving makand Harmonie and sound;
The fyre, the Air, the watter, and the ground –
Till understand it is aneuch, I wis,
That God in all his werkis wittie is.

Luke weill the fische that swimmis in the se;
Luke weill in eirth all kynd off bestiall;
The foulis ffair, sa forcelie thay fle,
Scheddand the air with pennis grit and small;
Syne luke to man, that he maid last off all,
Lyke to his Image and his similitude:
Be thir we knaw, that God is ffair and gude.

All Creature he maid ffor the behufe
Off man, and to his supportatioun
In to this eirth, baith under and abufe,
In number, wecht, and dew proportioun;
The difference off tyme, and ilk seasoun,
Concorddand till our opurtunitie,
As daylie by experience we may se.

sternis stars	*bestiall* beasts
cleir shining	*forcelie* strongly
till to	

The Somer with his Jolie mantill off grene,
With flouris fair furrit on everilk fent,
Quhilk Flora Goddes, off the flouris Quene,
Hes to that Lord as ffor his seasoun sent,
And Phebus with his goldin bemis gent
Hes purfellit and payntit plesandly,
With heit and moysture stilland ffrom the sky.

Syne Harvest hait, quhen Ceres that Goddes
Hir barnis benit hes with abundance;
And Bachus, God off wyne, renewit hes
The tume Pyipis in Italie and France,
With wynis wicht, and liquour off plesance;
And *Copia temporis* to fill hir horne,
That never wes full off quheit nor uther corne.

Syne wynter wan, quhen Austerne Eolus,
God off the wynd, with blastis boreall,
The grene garment off Somer glorious
Hes all to rent and revin in pecis small;
Than flouris fair faidit with froist man fall,
And birdis blyith changit thair noitis sweit
In styll murning, neir slane with snaw and sleit.

Thir dalis deip with dubbis drounit is,
Baith hill and holt heillit with frostis hair;
And bewis bene laifit bair off blis,
Be wickit windis off the winter wair.
All wyld beistis than ffrom the bentis bair

furrit furred   *wicht* strong
fent vent (in mantle)   *dubbis* puddles
gent beautiful   *holt* wood
purfellit decorated   *heillit* hidden
stilland distilling   *hair* hoar
barnis barns   *bewis* boughs
benit filled

Drawis ffor dreid unto thair dennis deip,
Coucheand ffor cauld in coifis thame to keip.

Syne cummis Ver, quhen winter is away,
The Secretar off Somer with his Sell,
Quhen Columbie up keikis throw the clay,
Quhilk fleit wes befoir with froistes fell.
The Mavis and the Merle beginnis to mell;
The Lark on loft, with uther birdis haill,
Than drawis furth ffra derne, over doun and daill.

That samin seasoun, in to ane soft morning,
Rycht blyth that bitter blastis wer ago,
Unto the wod, to se the flouris spring,
And heir the Mavis sing and birdis mo,
I passit ffurth, syne lukit to and ffro,
To se the Soill that wes richt sessonabill,
Sappie, and to resave all seidis abill.

Moving thusgait, grit myrth I tuke in mynd,
Off lauboraris to se the besines,
Sum makand dyke, and sum the pleuch can wynd,
Sum sawand seidis fast ffrome place to place,
The Harrowis hoppand in the saweris trace:
It wes grit Joy to him that luifit corne,
To se thame laubour, baith at evin and morne.

coifis hollows	*mell* mate
Sell seal (of office)	*haill* altogether
Columbie columbine	*derne* hiding
keikis peeps	*samin* same
fleit wes was withered	*wynd* guide (the plough)
Mavis and Merle thrush and	
blackbird	

And as I baid under ane bank full bene,
In hart gritlie rejosit off that sicht,
Unto ane hedge, under ane Hawthorne grene,
Off small birdis thair come ane ferlie flicht,
And doun belyif can on the leifis licht,
On everilk syde about me quhair I stude,
Rycht mervellous, ane mekill multitude.

Amang the quhilks ane Swallow loud couth cry,
On that Hawthorne hie in the croip sittand:
'O ye Birdis on bewis, heir me by,
Ye sall weill knaw, and wyislie understand,
Quhair danger is, or perrell appeirand;
It is grit wisedome to provyde befoir,
It to deuoyd, ffor dreid it hurt yow moir.'

'Schir Swallow' (quod the Lark agane), and leuch,
'Quhat haif ye sene that causis yow to dreid?'
'Se ye yone Churll' (quod scho) 'beyond yone pleuch,
Fast sawand hemp, and gude linget seid?
Yone lint will grow in lytill tyme in deid,
And thairoff will yone Churll his Nettis mak,
Under the quhilk he thinkis us to tak.

'Thairfoir I reid we pas quhen he is gone,
At evin, and with our naillis scharp and small
Out off the eirth scraip we yone seid anone,
And eit it up; ffor, giff it growis, we sall
Have cause to weip heirefter ane and all:
Se we remeid thairfoir ffurth with Instante,
Nam leuius lædit quicquid prævidimus ante.

ferlie sudden
croip tree-top
linget seid linseed

nam leuius, etc. for whatever
we have foreseen hurts us
more lightly

'For Clerkis sayis it is nocht sufficient
To considder that is befoir thyne Ee;
Bot prudence is ane inwart Argument,
That garris ane man prouyde and foirse
Quhat gude, quhat evill is liklie ffor to be,
Off everilk thing behald the fynall end,
And swa ffra perrell the better him defend.'

The Lark, lauchand, the Swallow thus couth scorne,
And said, scho fischit lang befoir the Net;
'The barne is eith to busk that is unborne;
All growis nocht that in the ground is set;
The nek to stoup, quhen it the straik sall get,
Is sone aneuch; deith on the fayest fall.'—
Thus scornit thay the Swallow ane and all.

Despysing thus hir helthsum document,
The foullis ferlie tuke thair flicht anone;
Sum with ane bir thay braidit over the bent,
And sum agane ar to the grene wod gone.
Upon the land quhair I wes left allone,
I tuke my club, and hamewart couth I carie,
Swa ferliand, as I had sene ane farie.

Thus passit furth quhill June, that Jolie tyde,
And seidis that wer sawin off beforne
Wer growin hie, that Hairis mycht thame hyde,
And als the Quailye craikand in the corne;
I movit furth, betwix midday and morne,
Unto the hedge under the Hawthorne grene,
Quhair I befoir the said birdis had sene.

barne child	*ferlie* quickly
eith easy	*bir* whirr
busk dress	*braidit* started quickly
fayest most fated (fey)	*carie* proceed
document warning	*swa ferliand* as wondering, as if

And as I stude, be aventure and cace,
The samin birdis as I haif said yow air,
I hoip, because it wes thair hanting place,
Mair off succour, or yit mair solitair,
Thay lychtit doun: and, quhen thay lychtit wair,
The Swallow swyth put furth ane pietuous pyme,
Said, 'wo is him can not bewar in tyme.

'O, blind birdis! and full off negligence,
Unmyndfull of your awin prosperitie,
Lift up your sicht, and tak gude advertence;
Luke to the Lint that growis on yone le;
Yone is the thing I bad forsuith that we,
Quhill it wes seid, suld rute furth off the eird;
Now is it Lint, now is it hie on breird.

'Go yit, quhill it is tender and small,
And pull it up; let it na mair Incres;
My flesche growis, my bodie quaikis all,
Thinkand on it I may not sleip in peis.'
Thay cryit all, and bad the Swallow ceis,
And said, 'yone Lint heirefter will do gude,
For Linget is to lytill birdis fude.

'We think, quhen that yone Lint bollis ar ryip,
To mak us Feist, and fill us off the seid,
Magre yone Churll, and on it sing and pyip.'
'Weill' (quod the Swallow), 'freindes hardilie beid;
Do as ye will, bot certane sair I dreid,
Heirefter ye sall find als sour, as sweit,
Quhen ye ar speldit on yone Carlis speit.

be aventure and cace by chance
said yow air mentioned to you before
swyth soon
pyme cry
on breird burgeoning
growis shudders
bollis pods
magre in spite of

'The awner off yone lint ane fouler is,
Richt cautelous and full off subteltie;
His pray full sendill tymis will he mis,
Bot giff we birdis all the warrer be;
Full mony off our kin he hes gart de,
And thocht it bot ane sport to spill thair blude:
God keip me ffra him, and the halie Rude.'

Thir small birdis haveand bot lytill thocht
Off perrell that micht fall be aventure,
The counsell off the Swallow set at nocht,
Bot tuke thair flicht, and furth togidder fure;
Sum to the wode, sum markit to the mure.
I tuke my staff, quhen this wes said and done,
And walkit hame, ffor it drew neir the none.

The Lint ryipit, the Carll pullit the Lyne,
Rippillit the bollis, and in beitis set,
It steipit in the burne, and dryit syne,
And with ane bittill knokkit it, and bet,
Syne swingillit it weill, and hekkillit in the flet;
His wyfe it span, and twynit it in to threid,
Of quhilk the Fowlar Nettis maid in deid.

The wynter come, the wickit wind can blaw,
The woddis grene were wallowit with the weit,
Baith firth and fell with froistys were maid faw,
Slonkis and slaik maid slidderie with the sleit;
The foulis ffair ffor falt thay ffell off feit;

cautelous treacherous	*bittill* club
sendill tymis seldom	*swingillit* scutched
fure set out	*hekkillit* combed
markit made for	*flet* inner part of house
mure moor	*faw* bright
rippillit removed the seeds	*slonkis, slaik* mires
beitis bundles	

On bewis bair it wes na bute to byde,
Bot hyit unto housis thame to hyde.

Sum in the barn, sum in the stak off corne
Thair lugeing tuke, and maid thair residence;
The Fowlar saw, and grit aithis hes sworne,
Thay suld be tane trewlie ffor thair expence.
His Nettis hes he set with diligence,
And in the snaw he schulit hes ane plane,
And heillit it all ouer with calf agane.

Thir small birdis seand the calff wes glaid;
Trowand it had bene corne, thay lychtit doun;
Bot of the Nettis na presume thay had,
Nor of the Fowlaris fals Intentioun;
To scraip, and seik thair meit thay maid thame boun.
The Swallow on ane lytill branche neir by,
Dreiddand for gyle, thus loud on thame couth cry:

'In to that calf scraip quhill your naillis bleid,
Thair is na corne, ye laubour all in vane;
Trow ye yone Churll for pietie will yow feid?
Na, na, he hes it heir layit for ane trane;
Remove, I reid, or ellis ye will be slane;
His Nettis he hes set full prively,
Reddie to draw; in tyme be war ffor thy.'

Grit fule is he that puttis in dangeir
His lyfe, his honour, ffor ane thing off nocht;
Grit fule is he, that will not glaidlie heir
Counsall in tyme, quhill it availl him nocht;
Grit fule is he, that hes na thing in thocht
Bot thing present, and efter quhat may fall,
Nor off the end hes na memoriall.

schulit shovelled   *calf* chaff
plane hollow space   *trane* snare
heillit covered   *ffor thy* of this

Thir small birdis ffor hunger famischit neir,
Full besie scraipand ffor to seik thair fude,
The counsall off the Swallow wald not heir,
Suppois thair laubour did thame lytill gude.
Quhen scho thair fulische hartis understude,
Sa Indurate, up in ane tre scho flew;
With that [this] Churll over thame his Nettis drew.

Allace! it wes grit hart sair for to se
That bludie Bowcheour beit thay birdis doun,
And ffor till heir, quhen thay wist weill to de,
Thair cairfull sang and lamentatioun:
Sum with ane staf he straik to eirth on swoun:
Off sum the heid he straik, off sum he brak the crag,
Sum half on lyfe he stoppit in his bag.

And quhen the Swallow saw that thay wer deid,
'Lo' (quod scho), 'thus it happinnis mony syis
On thame that will not tak counsall nor reid
Off Prudent men, or Clerkis that ar wyis;
This grit perrell I tauld thame mair than thryis;
Now ar thay deid, and wo is me thairfoir!'
Scho tuke hir flicht, bot I hir saw no moir.

MORALITAS

Lo, worthie folk, Esope, that Nobill clerk,
Ane Poet worthie to be Lawreate,
Quhen that he waikit from mair autentik werk,
With uther ma, this foirsaid Fabill wrate,
Quhilk at this tyme may weill be applicate
To guid morall edificatioun,
Haifand ane sentence, according to ressoun.

autentik proper

This Carll and bond of gentrice spoliate,
Sawand this calf, thir small birdis to sla,
It is the Feind, quhilk fra the Angelike state
Exylit is, as fals Apostata:
Quhilk day and nycht weryis not for to ga
Sawand poysoun in mony wickit thocht
In mannis Saull, quhilk Christ full deir hes bocht.

And quhen the saull, as seid in to the eird,
Gevis consent unto delectioun,
The wickit thocht beginnis for to breird
In deidlie sin, quhilk is dampnatioun;
Ressoun is blindit with affectioun,
And carnall lust grouis full grene and gay,
Throw consuetude hantit from day to day.

Proceding furth be use and consuetude,
The sin ryipis, and schame is set on syde;
The Feynd plettis his Nettis scharp and rude,
And under plesance previlie dois hyde;
Syne on the feild he sawis calf full wyde,
Quhilk is bot tume and verray vanitie
Of fleschlie lust, and vaine prosperitie.

Thir hungrie birdis wretchis we may call,
As scraipand in this warldis vane plesance,
Greddie to gadder gudis temporall,
Quhilk as the calf ar tume without substance,
Lytill of availl, and full of variance,
Lyke to the mow befoir the face of wind
Quhiskis away and makis wretchis blind.

bond husbandman
of gentrice spoliate entirely
   devoid of compassion
consuetude habit

hantit accustomed
tume empty
mow heap (of chaff)

This Swallow, quhilk eschaipit is the snair,
The halie Preichour weill may signifie,
Exhortand folk to walk and ay be wair
Fra Nettis of our wickit enemie,
Quha sleipis not, bot ever is reddie,
Quhen wretchis in this warld calf dois scraip,
To draw his Net, that thay may not eschaip.

Allace! quhat cair, quhat weiping is and wo,
Quhen Saull and bodie departit ar in twane!
The bodie to the wormis Keitching go,
The Saull to Fyre, to everlestand pane.
Quhat helpis than this calf, thir gudis vane,
Quhen thow art put in Luceferis bag,
And brocht to hell, and hangit be the crag?

Thir hid Nettis for to persave and se,
This sarie calf wyislie to understand,
Best is bewar in maist prosperite,
For in this warld thair is na thing lestand;
Is na man wait how lang his stait will stand,
His lyfe will lest, nor how that he sall end
Efter his deith, nor quhidder he sall wend.

Pray we thairfoir, quhill we ar in this lyfe,
For four thingis: the first, fra sin remufe;
The secund is fra all weir and stryfe;
The thrid is perfite cheritie and lufe;
The feird thing is, and maist for oure behufe,
That is in blis with Angellis to be fallow.
And thus endis the preiching of the Swallow.

Keitching kitchen   *fallow* companion
everlestand everlasting

The Taill of the Foxe, that begylit the Wolf, in the schadow of the Mone

In elderis dayis, as Esope can declair,
Thair wes ane Husband, quhilk had ane pleuch to steir.
His use wes ay in morning to ryse air;
Sa happinnit him in streiking tyme off yeir
Airlie in the morning to follow ffurth his feir,
Unto the pleuch, bot his gadman and he;
His stottis he straucht with 'Benedicite.'

The Caller cryit: 'how, haik, upon hicht;
Hald draucht, my dowis;' syne broddit thame ffull sair.
The Oxin wes unusit, young and licht,
And ffor fersnes thay couth the fur fforfair.
The Husband than woxe angrie as ane hair,
Syne cryit, and caist his Patill and grit stanis:
'The Wolff' (quod he) 'mot have yow all at anis.'

Bot yit the Wolff wes neirar nor he wend,
For in ane busk he lay, and Lowrence baith,
In ane Rouch Rone, wes at the furris end,
And hard the hecht; than Lowrence leuch full raith:
'To tak yone bud' (quod he) 'it wer na skaith.'

streiking tyme ploughing time	*wend* thought
feir companion (the driver)	*busk* bush
gadman goad-man, who on foot drove the team, while the other steered	*Lowrence* the fox
	Rouch rough
	Rone thicket
stottis oxen	*furris* furrow's
straucht urged on	*hecht* promise
Caller the driver	*raith* soon
haik go	*bud* bid, offer
Patill pattle, stick for clearing the coulter of stalks etc.	*skaith* damage

'Weill' (quod the Wolff), 'I hecht the be my hand;
Yone Carlliss word, as he wer King, sall stand.'

The Oxin waxit mair reullie at the last;
Syne efter thay lousit, ffra that it worthit weill lait;
The Husband hamewart with his cattell past.
Than sone the Wolff come hirpilland in his gait,
Befoir the Oxin, and schupe to mak debait.
The Husband saw him, and worthit sumdeill agast,
And bakwart with his beistis wald haif past.

The Wolff said, 'quhether dryvis thou this Pray?
I chalenge it, ffor nane off thame ar thyne.'
The man thairoff wes in ane felloun fray,
And soberlie to the Wolff answerit syne:
'Schir, be my Saull, thir oxin ar all myne;
Thairfoir I studdie quhy ye suld stop me,
Sen that I faltit never to you, trewlie.'

The Wolff said, 'Carle, gaif thou not me this drift
Airlie, quhen thou wes eirrand on yone bank?
And is thair oucht (sayis thou) frear than gift?
This tarying wyll tyne the all thy thank;
Far better is frelie ffor to giff ane plank
Nor be compellit on force to giff ane mart.
Fy on the fredome that cummis not with hart!'

reullie orderly
lousit unyoked
ffra that because
worthit weill lait was growing
    very late
hirpilland limping
schupe began

sumdeill somewhat
felloun terrible
fray fright
plank copper coin
mart fat ox
fredome generosity

'Schir' (quod the husband), 'ane man may say in greif,
And syne ganesay, fra he avise and se:
I hecht to steill, am I thairfoir ane theif?'
'God forbid, Schir, all hechtis suld haldin be!'
'Gaif I my hand or oblissing' (quod he),
'Or have ye witnes, or writ ffor to schaw?
Schir, reif me not, but go and seik the Law!'

'Carll' (quod the Wolff), 'ane Lord, and he be leill,
That schrinkis for schame, or doutis to be repruvit,
His saw is ay als sickker as his Seill.
Fy on the Leid that is not leill and lufit!
Thy argument is fals, and eik contrufit,
For it is said in Proverb: "But lawte
All uther vertewis ar nocht worth ane fle." '

'Schir,' said the husband, 'remember of this thing:
Ane leill man is not tane at halff ane taill.
I may say, and ganesay, I am na King:
Quhair is your witnes that hard I hecht thame haill?'
Than said the Wolff, 'thairfoir it sall nocht faill;
Lowrence' (quod he), 'cum hidder of that Schaw,
And say na thing bot as thow hard and saw.'

Lowrence come lourand, for he lufit never licht,
And sone appeirit befoir thame in that place:
The man leuch na thing, quhen he saw that sicht.
'Lowrence' (quod the Wolff), 'thow man declair this cace,
Quhairof we sall schaw the suith in schort space;
I callit on the leill witnes for to beir:
Quhat hard thow that this man hecht me lang eir?'

<hr>

oblissing obligation	*leill* honest
sickker sure	*taill* account
Leid man	*lourand* skulking

'Schir' (said the Tod), 'I can not hastelie
Swa sone as now gif sentence finall;
Bot wald ye baith submit yow heir to me,
To stand at my decreit perpetuall,
To pleis baith I suld preif, gif it may fall.'
'Weill' (quod the Wolf), 'I am content for me:'
The man said, 'swa am I, how ever it be.'

Than schew thay furth thair allegeance but fabill,
And baith proponit thair pley to him compleit.
(Quod Lowrence): 'now I am ane Juge amycabill:
Ye sall be sworne to stand at my decreit,
Quhether heirefter ye think it soure or sweit.'
The Wolff braid furth his fute, the man his hand,
And on the Toddis Taill sworne thay ar to stand.

Than tuke the Tod the man furth till ane syde,
And said him, 'friend, thow art in blunder brocht;
The Wolff will not forgif the ane Oxe hyde,
Yit wald my self fane help the, and I mocht;
Bot I am laith to hurt my conscience ocht.
Tyne nocht thy querrell in thy awin defence;
This will not throw but grit coist and expence.

'Seis thow not Buddis beiris Bernis throw,
And giftis garris crukit materis hald ffull evin?
Sumtymis ane hen haldis ane man in ane Kow.
All ar not halie that heifis thair handis to hevin.'
'Schir' (said the man), 'ye sall have sex or sevin,

decreit decree   *Buddis* bids, bribes
preif try   *beiris* carry
braid stretched   *Bernis* men
ane syde aside   *throw* through
and I mocht if I might   *garris* made

Richt off the fattest hennis off all the floik:
I compt not all the laif, leif me the Coik.'

'I am ane Juge' (quod Lowrence than), and leuch;
'Thair is na Buddis suld beir me by the rycht;
I may tak hennis and Caponis weill aneuch,
For God is gane to sleip; as ffor this nycht,
Sic small thingis ar not sene in to his sicht;
Thir hennis' (quod he) 'sall mak thy querrell sure,
With emptie hand na man suld Halkis lure.'

Concordit thus, than Lowrence tuke his leiff,
And to the Wolff he went in to ane ling;
Syne prevelie he plukkit him be the sleiff:
'Is this in ernist' (quod he) 'ye ask sic thing?
Na, be my Saull, I trow it be in heithing.'
Than saith the Wolff, 'Lowrence, quhy sayis thow sa?
Thow hard the hecht thy selff that he couth ma.'

'The hecht' (quod he) 'yone man maid at the pleuch,
Is that the cause quhy ye the cattell craif?'
Halff in to heithing (said Lowrence than), and leuch;
'Schir, be the Rude, unroikit now ye raif;
The Devill ane stirk taill thairfoir sall ye haif;
Wald I tak it upon my conscience
To do sa pure ane man as yone offence?

---

laif rest
Coik cock
querrell legal case
Halkis hawks
ling patch of heather

heithing mockery
couth ma did make
unroikit unbalanced
pure poor

'Yit haif I communit with the Carll' (quod he);
'We ar concordit upon this cunnand:
Quyte off all clamis, swa ye will mak him fre,
Ye sall ane Cabok have in to your hand,
That sic ane sall not be in all this land;
For it is Somer Cheis, baith fresche and ffair;
He sayis it weyis ane stane, and sumdeill mair.'

'Is that thy counsell' (quod the Wolff), 'I do,
That yone Carll ffor ane Cabok suld be fre?'
'Ye, be my Saull, and I wer sworne yow to,
Ye suld nane uther counsell have for me;
For gang ye to the maist extremitie,
It will not wyn yow worth ane widderit neip;
Schir, trow ye not, I have ane Saull to keip?'

'Weill' (quod the Wolff), 'it is aganis my will
That yone Carll for ane Cabok suld ga quyte.'
'Schir' (quod the Tod), 'ye tak it in nane evill,
For, be my Saull, your self had all the wyte.'
'Than' (said the Wolf) 'I bid na mair to flyte,
Bot I wald se yone Cabok off sic pryis.'
'Schir' (said the Tod), 'he tauld me quhar it lyis.'

Than hand in hand thay held unto ane hill;
The Husband till his hors hes tane the way,
For he wes fane; he schaipit ffrom thair ill,
And on his feit woke the dure quhill day.
Now will we turne vnto the uther tway.
Throw woddis waist thir Freikis on fute can fair,
Fra busk to busk, quhill neir midnycht and mair.

cunnand covenant,   *quyte* quit
   understanding   *Cabok* cheese

Lowrence wes ever remembring upon wrinkis
And subtelteis the Wolff for to begyle;
That he had hecht ane Caboik, he forthinkis,
Yit at the last he findis furth ane wyle,
Than at him selff softlie couth he smyle.
The Wolff sayis, 'Lowrence, thow playis bellie blind;
We seik all nycht, bot na thing can we find.'

'Schir' (said the Tod), 'we ar at it almaist;
Soft yow ane lytill, and ye sall se it sone.'
Than to ane Manure place thay hyit in haist:
The nicht wes lycht, and pennyfull the Mone.
Than till ane draw well thir Senyeours past but hone,
Quhair that twa bukkettis severall suithlie hang;
As ane come up, ane uther doun wald gang.

The schadow of the Mone schone in the well.
'Schir' (said Lowrence), 'anis ye sall find me leill;
Now se ye not the Caboik weill your sell,
Quhyte as ane Neip, and round als as ane seill?
He hang it yonder, that na man suld it steill:
Schir, traist ye weill, yone Caboik ye se hing
Micht be ane present to ony Lord or King.'

'Na' (quod the Wolff) 'mycht I yone Caboik haif
On the dry land, as I it yonder se,
I wald quitclame the Carll of all the laif;
His dart Oxin I compt thame not ane fle;
Yone wer mair meit for sic ane man as me.
Lowrence' (quod he), 'leip in the bukket sone,
And I sall hald the ane, quhill thow have done.'

schadow reflection   *dart* draught
seill seal

Lowrence gird doun baith sone and subtellie;
The uther baid abufe, and held the flaill.
'It is sa mekill' (quod Lowrence) 'it maisteris me,
On all my tais it hes not left ane naill;
Ye man mak help upwart, and it haill
Leip in the uther bukket haistelie,
And cum sone doun, and make me sum supple.'

Than lychtlie in the bukket lap the loun;
His wecht but weir the uther end gart ryis;
The Tod come hailland up, the Wolf yeid doun;
Than angerlie the Wolff upon him cryis:
'I cummand thus dounwart, quhy thow upwart hyis?'
'Schir' (quod the Foxe), 'thus fairis it off Fortoun:
As ane cummis up, scho quheillis ane uther doun!'

Than to the ground sone yeid the Wolff in haist;
The Tod lap on land, als blyith as ony bell,
And left the Wolff in watter to the waist.
Quha haillit him out, I wait not, off the well.
Heir endis he Text; thair is na mair to tell.
Yit men may find ane gude moralitie
In this sentence, thocht it ane Fabill be.

MORALITAS

This Wolff I likkin to ane wickit man,
Quhilk dois the pure oppres in everie place,
And pykis at thame all querrellis that he can,
Be Rigour, reif, and uther wickitnes.
The Foxe the Feind I call in to this cais,

gird went	*tais* toes
baid stayed	*supple* help
flaill beater	*pykis* picks

Actand ilk man to ryn unrychteous rinkis,
Thinkand thairthrow to lok him in his linkis.

The Husband may be callit ane godlie man,
With quhome the Feynd falt findes (as Clerkis reids),
Besie to tempt him with all wayis that he can.
The hennis ar warkis that fra ferme faith proceidis:
Quhair sic sproutis spreidis, the evill spreit thair not speids,
Bot wendis vnto the wickit man agane;
That he hes tint his travell is full unfane.

The wodds waist, quhairin wes the Wolff wyld,
Ar wickit riches, quhilk all men gaipis to get;
Quha traistis in sic Trusterie ar oft begyld;
For Mammon may be callit the Devillis Net,
Quhilk Sathanas for all sinfull hes set.
With proud plesour quha settis his traist thairin,
But speciall grace, lychtlie can not outwin.

The Cabok may be callit Covetyce,
Quhilk blomis braid in mony mannis Ee;
Wa worth the well of that wickit vyce!
For it is all bot fraud and fantasie,
Dryvand ilk man to leip in the buttrie
That dounwart drawis unto the pane of hell. –
Christ keip all Christianis from that wickit well!

actand actuating	*unfane* frustrated
ryn . . . rinkis perform . . . deeds	*Trusterie* securities
thairthrow thereby	*lychtlie* easily
ferme firm	*wa worth . . .* evil to . . .!
sproutis good seed	*buttrie* larder
travell work	

Robene and Makyne

Robene sat on gud grene hill,
Kepand a flok of fe:
mirry makyne said him till,
'Robene, thow rew on me;
I haif the luvit lowd and still,
Thir yeiris two or thre;
my dule in dern bot gif thow dill,
Dowtless but dreid I de.'

Robene ansert, 'be the rude,
nathing of lufe I knaw,
Bot keipis my scheip undir yone wid,
Lo quhair thay raik on raw:
quhat hes marrit the in thy mude,
makyne, to me thow schaw;
Or quhat is lufe, or to be lude?
Fane wald I leir that law.'

'At luvis lair gife thow will leir,
Tak thair ane a b c:
be heynd, courtass, and fair of feir,
Wyse, hardy, and fre;
So that no denger do the deir,
quhat dule in dern thow dre;

fe sheep	*marrit* marred
rew have pity	*lude* loved
lowd, etc. openly and secretly	*lair* lore
dule, etc. my hidden woe unless you share	*heynd* gentle
dowtless, etc. I shall certainly die	*feir* manner
raik on raw range in row	*deir* frighten
	dre endure

preiss the with pane at all poweir,
be patient and previe.'

Robene anserit hir agane,
'I wait not quhat is luve;
Bot I haif mervell incertane
Quhat makis the this wanrufe:
The weddir is fair, & I am fane,
my scheip gois haill aboif;
And we wald play us in this plane,
They wald us bayth reproif.'

'Robene, tak tent unto my taill,
And wirk all as I reid,
And thow sall haif my hairt all haill,
Eik and my madinheid.
Sen god sendis bute for baill,
And for murning remeid,
I dern with the, bot gif I daill,
Dowtles I am bot deid.'

'Makyne, to morne this ilk a tyde,
And ye will meit me heir,
Peraventure my scheip ma gang besyd,
quhill we haif liggit full neir;
Bot mawgre haif I and I byd,
Fra thay begin to steir;
quhat lyis on hairt I will not hyd;
Makyn, than mak gud cheir.'

eik *and* and also
bute for baill cure for grief
daill deal, dally
ilk a tyde same time
liggit lain

mawgre ill-will
byd remain, linger
fra from the time that
steir stir

'Robene, thow reivis me roif and rest;
I luve bot the allone.'
'Makyne, adew, the sone gois west,
The day is neir hand gone.'
'Robene, in dule I am so drest,
That lufe wilbe my bone.'
'Ga lufe, makyne, quhair evir thow list,
ffor lemman I [bid] none.'

'Robene, I stand in sic a styll;
I sicht, and that full sair.'
'Makyne, I haif bene heir this quhyle;
at hame god gif I wair.'
'my huny, robene, talk ane quhill,
gif thow will do na mair.'
'Makyne, sum uthir man begyle,
ffor hamewart I will fair.'

Robene on his wayis went,
als licht as leif of tre;
mawkin murnit in hir intent,
and trowd him nevir to se.
Robene brayd attour the bent;
Than mawkyne cryit on hie,
'Now ma thow sing, for I am schent!
quhat alis lufe at me?'

reivis robs
roif peace
drest smothered
bone death, doom
styll state

sicht sighed
wair were
brayd, etc. strode across the moor
hie aloud

Mawkyne went hame withowttin faill,
Full wery eftir cowth weip:
Than robene in a fulfair daill
Assemblit all his scheip.
Be that sum pairte of mawkynis aill
Outthrow his hairt cowd creip;
he fallowit hir fast thair till assaill,
and till hir tuke gude keip.

'Abyd, abyd, thow fair makyne,
a word for ony thing;
For all my luve it salbe thyne,
Withowttin depairting.
all haill, thy harte for till haif myne
Is all my cuvating;
my scheip to morne quhill houris nyne
Will neid of no keping.'

'Robene, thow hes hard soung & say,
In gestis and storeis auld,
The man that will nocht quhen he may
sall haif nocht quhen he wald.
I pray to Jesu every day
mot eik thair Cairis cauld,
that first preiss with the to play,
be firth, forrest, or fawld.'

'Makyne, the nicht is soft and dry,
The wedder is warme & fair,
And the grene woid rycht neir us by
To walk attour all quhair;

eftir, *etc*. like to weep   *fawld* pasture
firth field

Thair ma na Janglour us espy,
That is to lufe contrair;
Thairin, makyne, bath ye & I
Unsene we may repair.'

'Robene, that warld is all away
and quyt brocht till ane end,
and nevir agane thairto perfay
Sall it be as thow wend;
For of my pane thow maid it play,
and all in vane I spend;
as thow hes done, sa sall I say,
murne on, I think to mend.'

'Mawkyne, the howp of all my heill,
my hairt on the is sett,
and evirmair to the be leill,
quhill I may leif but lett;
nevir to faill, as utheris feill,
quhat grace that evir I gett.'
'Robene, with the I will nocht deill;
Adew, for thus we mett.'

Malkyne went hame blyth annewche,
Attour the holttis hair;
Robene murnit, and Malkyne lewche;
Scho sang, He sichit sair;
and so left him, bayth wo & wrewche,
In dolour & in cair,
Kepand his hird under a huche,
amangis the holtis hair.

Janglour slanderer   *feill* fail
perfay by faith   *annewche* enough
wend desire   *attour*, *etc.* over the grey hills
heill well-being   *lewche* laughed
leill loyal   *huche* cliff
but lett without hindrance

The Abbay Walk

Allone as I went up and doun
in ane abbay was fair to se,
Thinkand quhat consolatioun
Was best in to adversitie,
On caiss I kest on syd myne E,
And saw this writtin upoun a wall:
'off quhat estait, man, that thow be,
Obey and thank thy god of all.

'Thy kindome and thy grit empyre,
Thy ryaltie, nor riche array,
Sall nocht endeur at thy desyre,
Bot as the wind will wend away;
Thy gold and all thy gudis gay,
quhen fortoun list will fra the fall;
Sen thow sic sampillis seis ilk day,
Obey and thank thy god of all.

'Job wes maist riche in writ we find,
Thobe maist full of cheritie:
Job woux pure, and thobe blynd,
Bath tempit with adversitie.
Sen blindness wes infirmitie,
and poverty wes naturall,
Thairfoir rycht patiently bath he and he
Obeyid and thankit god of all.

on caiss by chance   *tempit* tempted
sampillis examples

'Thocht thow be blind, or haif ane halt,
Or in thy face deformit ill,
Sa it cum nocht throw thy defalt,
Na man suld the repreif by skill.
Blame nocht thy Lord, sa is his will;
Spurn nocht thy fute aganis the wall;
Bot with meik hairt and prayer still
obey, &c.

'God of his justice mon correct,
and of his mercy petie haif;
he is ane Juge to nane suspect,
To puneiss synfull man and saif.
Thocht thow be lord attour the laif,
and eftirwart maid bound and thrall,
ane pure begger, with skrip and staif,
obey, &c.

'This changeing and grit variance
off erdly staitis up and doun
Is nocht bot causualitie and chance,
as sum men sayis, without ressoun,
Bot be the grit provisioun
of god aboif that rewll the sall;
Thairfoir evir thow mak the boun
To obey, &c.

'In welth be meik, heich nocht thy self;
be glaid in wilfull povertie;
Thy power and thy warldis pelf
Is nocht bot verry vanitie.

repreif reprove   *boun* ready
attour above   *heich* elevate
laif others

Remember him that deit on tre,
For thy saik taistit the bittir gall;
quha heis law hairtis and lawis he;
obey and thank thy god of all.'

The Taill of the Uponlandis Mous, and the Burges Mous

Esope, myne Authour, makis mentioun
Of twa myis and thay wer Sisteris deir,
Of quham the eldest dwelt in ane Borous toun,
The uther wynnit uponland weill neir;
Soliter, quhyle under busk, quhyle under breir,
Quhilis in the corne, and uther mennis skaith,
As outlawis dois, and levis on their waith.

This rurall mous in to the wynter tyde,
Had hunger, cauld, and tholit grit distress;
The uther Mous, that in the Burgh can byde,
Was Gild brother and made ane fre Burges;
Toll fre als, but custom mair or les,
And fredome had to ga quhair ever scho list,
Amang the cheis in Ark, and meill in kist.

Ane tyme when scho was full and unfute sair,
Scho tuke in mynd hir sister uponland,
And langit for to heir of hir weilfair,
To se quhat lyfe scho had under the wand.
Bairfute, allone, with pykestaf in hir hand,
As pure pylgryme scho passit out off town,
To seik hir sister baith oure daill and down.

wynnit dwelt
uponland in the countryside
busk bush
skaith harm
waith cunning

tholit suffered
but custom tax free
kist chest
wand rod

Furth mony wilsum wayis can scho walk,
Throw mosse and mure, throw bankis, busk & breir,
Scho ran cryand, quhill scho came to a balk:
'Cum furth to me, my awin Sister deir,
Cry peip anis!' With that the Mous culd heir,
And knew hir voce as kinnisman will do,
Be verray kynd; and furth scho come hir to.

The hartlie joy, God! geve ye had sene,
Beis kith quhen that thir Sisteris met;
And grit kyndnes wes schawin thame betwene,
For quhylis thay leuch, and quhylis for joy thay gret,
Quhyle(s) kissit sweit, quhylis in armis plet;
And thus thay fure quhill soberit wes thair mude,
Syne ffute ffor ffute unto the chalmer yude.

As I hard say, it was ane sober wane,
Off fog & farne ffull febilie wes maid,
Ane sillie scheill under ane steidfast stane,
Off quhilk the entres wes not hie nor braid.
And in the samin thay went but mair abaid,
Without fyre or candill birnand bricht,
For comonly sic pykeris luffis not lycht.

Quhen thay wer lugit thus, thir sely Myse,
The youngest sister into hir butterie glyde,
And brocht furth nuttis, & candill in steid off spyce;
Giff this wes gude ffair I do it on thame besyde.
The Burges Mous prompit forth in pryde,

wilsum bewildering, wild	*fure* fared
balk field	*yude* went
anis once	*fog* foliage
kynd family likeness	*scheill* shelter
hartlie cordial	*abaid* abiding, delay
beis kith was shown	*pykeris* pilferers
gret wept	*sely, selie* harmless

And said, 'sister, is this your dayly fude?'
'Quhy not,' quod scho, 'is not this meit rycht gude?'

'Na, be my saull, I think it bot ane scorne.'
'Madame' (quod scho), 'ye be the mair to blame;
My mother sayd, sister, quhen we wer borne,
That I and ye lay baith within ane wame.
I keip the rate and custome off my dame,
And off my leving into povertie,
For landis have we nane in propertie.'

'My fair sister' (quod scho), 'have me excusit.
This rude dyat and I can not accord.
To tender meit my stomok is ay usit,
For quhylis I fair alsweill as ony Lord.
Thir wydderit peis, and nuttis, or thay be bord,
Wil brek my teith, and mak my wame fful sklender,
Quhilk wes before usit to meitis tender.'

'Weil, weil, sister' (quod the rurall Mous),
'Geve it pleis yow, sic thing as ye se heir,
Baith meit and dreink, harberie and hous,
Salbe your awin, will ye remane al yeir.
Ye sall it have wyth blyith and mery cheir,
And that suld mak the maissis that ar rude,
Amang freindis, richt tender and wonder gude.

'Quhat plesure is in the ffeistis delicate,
The quhilkis ar gevin with ane glowmand brow?
Ane gentill hart is better recreate
With blyith curage, than seith to him ane Kow.
Ane modicum is mair ffor till allow,

wame womb, abdomen   *or* before
rate standard   *harberie* lodging

Swa that gude will be kerver at the dais,
Than thrawin vult and mony spycit mais.'

For all hir mery exhortatioun,
This Burges Mous had littill will to sing.
Bot hevilie scho kest hir browis doun,
For all the daynteis that scho culd hir bring.
Yit at the last scho said, halff in hething,
'Sister, this victuall and your royall feist,
May weill suffice unto ane rurall beist.

'Lat be this hole and cum into my place;
I sall to you schaw be experience
My gude friday is better nor your pace;
My dische likingis is worth your haill expence.
I have housis anew off grit defence;
Off cat, nor fall trap, I have na dreid.'
'I grant,' quod scho; and on togidder thay yeid.

In stubbill array throw gers and corne,
And under buskis prevelie couth thay creip,
The eldest wes the gyde and went beforne,
The younger to hir wayis tuke gude keip.
On nicht thay ran, and on the day can sleip,
Quhill in the morning, or the Laverok sang,
Thay fand the town, and in blythlie couth gang.

Not fer fra thyne unto ane worthie Wane,
This Burges brocht thame sone quhare thay suld be,
Without God speid thair herberie wes tane,
In to ane spence with vittell grit plentie;
Baith Cheis and Butter upon thair skelfis hie,

thrawin twisted	*Laverok* lark
vult visage	*Wane* dwelling
hething scorn	*spence* larder
pace Easter feast	*skelfis* shelves
yeid went	*hie* high

And flesche and fische aneuch, baith fresche and salt,
And sekkis full off meill and eik off malt.

Eftir quhen thay disposit wer to dyne,
Withowtin grace thay wesche and went to meit,
With all coursis that Cukis culd devyne,
Muttoun and beif, strikin in tailyeis greit.
Ane Lordis fair thus couth thay counterfeit,
Except ane thing, thay drank the watter cleir
In steid off wyne, bot yit thay maid gude cheir.

With blyith upcast and merie countenance,
The eldest Sister sperit at hir gest
Giff that scho be ressone fand difference
Betwix that chalmer and hir sarie nest.
'Ye, dame' (quod scho), 'how lang will this lest?'
'For evermair, I wait, and langer to.'
'Giff it be swa, ye ar at eis' (quod scho).

Till eik thair cheir ane subcharge furth scho brocht,
Ane plait off grottis, and ane dische full off meill;
Thraf cakkis als I trow scho spairit nocht,
Aboundantlie about hir for to deill.
And mane full fyne scho brocht in steid off geill,
And ane quhyte candill out off ane coffer stall,
In steid off spyce to gust thair mouth withall.

wesche washed	*subcharge* second course
tailyeis slices	*grottis* husked oats
upcast raillery	*thraf cakkis* wheaten cakes
wait know	*mane* fine bread
swa so	*geill* jelly
till eik to add to	*stall* stolen

This maid thay merie quhill thay micht na mair
And 'haill yule, haill!' cryit upon hie;
Yit efter joy oftymes cummis cair,
And troubill efter grit prosperitie.
Thus as thay sat in all thair jolitie,
The spenser come with keyis in his hand,
Oppinnit the dure, and thame at denner fand.

Thay taryit not to wesche, as I suppose,
Bot on to ga quha that micht fformest win.
The Burges had ane hole, and in scho gois,
Hir sister had na hole to hyde hir in:
To se that selie Mous it wes grit sin,
So desolate and will off ane gude reid,
For verray dreid scho fell in swoun neir deid.

Bot as God wald, it fell ane happie cace,
The Spenser had na laser for to byde,
Nowther to seik, nor serche, to sker nor chace,
Bot on he went, and left the dure up wyde.
The bald Burges his passing weill hes spyde,
Out off hir hole scho come, and cryit on hie,
'How fair ye, sister? cry peip, quhair ever ye be.'

This rurall Mous lay flatling on the ground,
And for the deith scho wes full sair dredand,
For till hir hart straik mony wofull stound,
As in ane fever scho trimbillit fute and hand.
And quhan her sister in sic ply hir fand,
For verray pietie scho began to greit,
Syne confort hir with wordis hunny sweit.

spenser butler	*dure* door
win attain	*ply* plight
and will, etc. at a loss for good	*greit* weep
counsel	

'Quhy ly ye thus? ryse up, my sister deir,
Cum to your meit, this perrell is overpast.'
The uther answerit hir with hevie cheir,
'I may not eit, sa sair I am agast;
I had lever thir fourty dayis fast,
With watter caill, and to gnaw benis or peis,
Than all your feist in this dreid and diseis.'

With fair tretie yit scho gart hir upryse,
And to the burde thay went and togidder sat,
And scantlie had thay drunkin anis or twyse,
Quhen in come Gib hunter, our Jolie Cat,
And bad God speid; the Burges up with that,
And till her hole scho went as fyre on flint;
Bawdronis the uther be the bak hes hint.

Fra fute to fute he kest hir to and ffra,
Quhylis up, quhylis doun, als cant as ony kid;
Quhylis wald he lat hir rin under the stra,
Quhylis wald he wink, and play with hir buk heid.
Thus to the selie Mous grit pane he did,
Quhill at the last, throw fortune and gude hap,
Betwix ane burde and the wall scho crap.

And up in haist behind ane parraling
Scho clam so hie, that Gilbert micht not get hir,
Syne be the cluke thair craftelie can hing,
Till he wes gane, hir cheir wes all the better.
Syne doun scho lap quhen thair wes nane to let hir,

lever rather	*stra* straw
watter caill cabbage water	*buk heid* hide and seek
gart made, caused	*crap* crept
Bawdronis cat	*parraling* partition
hint seized	*cluke* claw
cant playful	*let* prevent

And to the Burges Mous loud can scho cry,
'Fairweill, sister, thy feist heir I defy!

'Thy mangerie is mingit all with cair,
Thy guse is gude, thy gansell sour as gall.
The subcharge off thy service is bot sair,
Sa sall thow find heir efterwart na ffall.
I thank yone courtyne and yone perpall wall
Of my defence now ffra yone crewall beist.
Almichtie God, keip me fra sic ane ffeist!

'Wer I into the kith that I come ffra,
For weill nor wo, suld I never cum agane.'
With that scho tuke her leif and furth can ga,
Quhylis throw the corne, and quhylis throw the plane;
Quhen scho wes furth and fre scho wes full fane,
And merilie markit unto the mure.
I can not tell how weill thairefter scho fure.

Bot I hard say scho passit to hir den,
Als warme as woll, suppose it wes not greit,
Full beinly stuffit, baith but and ben,
Off Beinis, and Nuttis, peis, Ry, and Quheit.
Quhen ever scho list, scho had aneuch to eit,
In quyet and eis withoutin ony dreid;
Bot to hir sisteris feist na mair scho yeid.

MORALITAS

Freindis, ye may find, and ye will tak heid,
In to this fabill ane gude moralitie.
As fitchis myngit ar with nobill seid,
Swa interminglit is adversitie

mangerie feasting	*perpall* partition
mingit mingled	*kith* home
gansell sauce	*markit* marched, rode

With eirdlie joy, swa that na estate is frie,
Without trubill and sum vexatioun:
And namelie thay quhilk clymmis up maist hie,
That ar not content with small possessioun.

Blissed be sempill lyfe withoutin dreid;
Blissed be sober feist in quietie;
Quha hes aneuch, of na mair hes he neid,
Thocht it be littill into quantatie.
Grit aboundance and blind prosperitie
Oftymes makis ane evill conclusioun:
The sweitest lyfe thairfoir, in this cuntrie,
Is sickernes with small possessioun.

O wanton man! that usis for to feid
Thy wambe, and makis it a God to be,
Lieke to thy self; I warne the weill but dreid,
The Cat cummis, and to the Mous hes Ee.
Quhat vaillis than thy feist and royaltie,
With dreidfull hart, and tribulatioun?
Best thing in eird, thairfoir, I say, for me,
Is blyithnes in hart, with small possessioun.

Thy awin fyre, my freind, sa it be bot ane gleid,
It warmis weill, and is worth Gold to the.
And Solomon sayis, gif that thow will reid,
'Under the hevin thair can not better be,
Than ay be blyith and leif in honestie.'
Quhairfoir I may conclude be this ressoun:
Of eirthly joy it beiris maist degre,
Blyithnes in hart, with small possessioun.

sickernes security   gleid spark
wambe stomach

The Prais of Aige

Wythin a garth, under a rede rosere,
Ane ald man, and decrepit, herd I syng;
Gay was the note, suete was the voce et clere:
It was grete joy to here of sik a thing.
'And to my dome,' he said, in his dytyng,
'For to be yong I wald not, for my wis
Off all this warld to mak me lord et king:
The more of age the nerar hevynnis blis.

'False is this warld, and full of variance,
Besoucht with syn and other sytis mo;
Treuth is all tynt, gyle has the gouvernance,
Wrechitnes has wroht all welthis wele to wo;
Fredome is tynt, and flemyt the lordis fro,
And covatise is all the cause of this;
I am content that youthede is ago:
The more of age the nerar hevynnis blisse.

'The state of youth I repute for na gude,
For in that state sik perilis now I see;
Bot full smal grace, the regeing of his blude
Can none gaynstand quhill that he agit be;
Syne of the thing that tofore joyit he
Nothing remaynis for to be callit his;
For quhy it were bot veray vanitee:
The more of age the nerar hevynnis blisse.

'Suld no man traist this wrechit warld, for quhy
Of erdly joy ay sorow is the end;
The state of it can noman certify,
This day a king, to morne na gude to spend.
Quhat have we here bot grace us to defend?
The quhilk god grant us for to mend oure mys,
That to his glore he may oure saulis send;
The more of age the nerar hevynnis blisse.'

The Bludy Serk

This hindir yeir I hard be tald
Thair was a worthy king;
Dukis, erlis, and barronis bald
He had at his bidding.
The lord was anceane and ald,
And sexty yeiris cowth ring;
he had a dochter fair to fald,
a Lusty Lady ying.

Off all fairheid scho bur the flour,
And eik hir faderis air,
Off lusty laitis and he honour,
Meik bot and debonair.
Scho wynnit in a bigly bour;
On fold wes none so fair;
princis luvit hir paramour,
In cuntreis our all quhair.

Thair dwelt alyt besyde the king
A fowll gyane of ane;
stollin he hes the lady ying,
away with hir is gane,
and kest hir in his dungering,
Quhair licht scho micht se nane;
hungir and cauld and grit thristing
Scho fand in to hir wame.

He wes the laithliest on to luk
that on the ground mycht gang;
His nailis wes lyk ane hellis cruk,
Thairwith fyve quarteris lang.

Thair wes nane that he ourtuk,
In rycht or yit in wrang,
Bot all in schondir he thame schuke –
The gyane wes so strang.

He held the lady day and nycht
Within his deip dungeoun;
he wald nocht gif of hir a sicht,
for gold nor yit ransoun,
Bot gife the king mycht get a knycht,
To fecht with his persoun –
To fecht with him both day and nycht,
Quhill ane wer dungin doun.

The king gart seik baith fer and neir,
beth be se and land,
off ony knycht gife he micht heir
wald fecht with that gyand.
a worthy prince that had no peir
hes tane the deid on hand,
For the luve of the Lady cleir,
and held full trew cunnand.

That prince come prowdly to the toun
of that gyane to heir,
and fawcht with him his awin persoun,
and tuke him presoneir;
And kest him In his awin dungeoun,
allane withouttin feir,
With hungir, cauld, and confusioun,
As full weill worthy weir.

Syne brak the bour, had hame the bricht,
Unto hir fadir deir;
Sa evill wondit was the knycht
That he behuvit to de.
Unlusum was his likame dicht,
His sark was all bludy;
In all the warld was thair a wicht
So peteouss for to sy?

The lady murnyt and maid grit mone,
With all hir mekle micht:
'I luvit nevir lufe bot one,
that dulfully now is dicht.
God sen my lyfe were fra me tone,
or I had sene yone sicht,
or ellis in begging evir to gone
furth with yone curtass knycht.'

he said, 'fair lady, now mone I
De, trestly ye me trow;
Tak ye my sark that is bludy,
and hing It forrow yow;
first think on it, and syne on me,
quhen men cumis yow to wow.'
The lady said, 'be mary fre,
Thairto I mak a wow.'

Quhen that scho lukit to the serk,
Scho thocht on the persoun,
and prayit for him with all hir harte,
That Lowsd hir of bandoun,
quhair scho was wont to sit full merk
In that deip dungeoun;
and evir quhill scho wes in quert,
That wass hir a lessoun.

Sa weill the lady luvit the knycht,
that no man wald scho tak.
Sa suld we do our god of micht,
That did all for us mak;
quhilk fullely to deid wes dicht
for sinfull manis saik;
Sa suld we do both day and nycht,
With prayaris to him mak.

MORALITAS

This king is lyk the trinitie,
Baith in hevin and heir;
The manis saule to the Lady;
The gyane to Lucefeir;
The knycht to chryst, that deit on tre,
And coft our synnis deir;
The pit to hell, with panis fell;
The syn to the woweir.

The lady was wowd, bot scho said nay,
With men that wald hir wed;
Sa suld we wryth all syn away,
That in our breistis bred.
I pray to Jesu chryst verrey,
For us his blud that bled,
To be our help on domysday,
quhair lawis are straitly led.

The saule is godis dochtir deir,
And eik his handewerk,
That was betrasit with lucifeir,
quha sittis in hell full merk.
Borrowit with chrystis angell cleir,
hend men, will ye nocht herk?
ffor his lufe that bocht us deir,
Think on the bludy serk.

The Garmont of Gud Ladeis

Wald my gud lady lufe me best,
and wirk eftir my will,
I suld ane garmond gudliest
Gar mak hir body till.

Off he honour suld be hir hud,
upoun hir heid to weir,
garneist with governance so gud,
na demyng suld hir deir.

Hir sark suld be hir body nixt,
Of chestetie so quhyt,
With schame and Dreid togidder mixt,
The same suld be perfyt.

Hir kirtill suld be of clene constance,
Lasit with lesum Lufe,
The mailyeis of continwance
for nevir to remufe.

Hir gown suld be of gudliness,
Weill ribband with renowne,
Purfillit with plesour in ilk place,
furrit with fyne fassoun.

Hir belt suld be of benignitie,
Abowt hir middill meit;
Hir mantill of humilitie,
To tholl bayth wind & weit.

Hir hat suld be of fair having,
And hir tepat of trewth;
Hir patelet of gud pansing;
Hir hals ribbane of rewth.

Hir slevis suld be of esperance,
To keip hir fra dispair;
hir gluvis of gud govirnance,
to gyd hir fyngearis fair.

Hir schone suld be of sickernes,
In syne that scho nocht slyd;
Hir hoiss of honestie, I ges,
I suld for hir provyd.

Wald scho put on this garmond gay,
I durst sweir by my seill,
That scho woir nevir grene nor gray
That set hir half so weill.

More about Penguins

Penguinews, which appears every month, contains details of all the new books issued by Penguins as they are published. From time to time it is supplemented by *Penguins in Print*, which is a complete list of all available books published by Penguins. (There are well over three thousand of these.)

A specimen copy of *Penguinews* will be sent to you free on request, and you can become a subscriber for the price of the postage. For a year's issues (including the complete lists) please send 3op if you live in the United Kingdom, or 6op if you live elsewhere. Just write to Dept EP, Penguin Books Ltd, Harmondsworth, Middlesex, enclosing a cheque or postal order, and your name will be added to the mailing list.

Note: *Penguinews* and *Penguins in Print* are not available in the U.S.A. or Canada

Poet to Poet

The response of one poet to the work of another can be doubly illuminating. In each volume of this new Penguin series a living poet presents his own edition of the work of a British or American poet of the past. By their choice of poet, by their selection of verses, and by the personal and critical reactions they express in their introductions, the poets of today thus provide an intriguing insight into themselves and their own work whilst reviving interest in poetry they have particularly admired.

Already published:
Crabbe by C. Day Lewis
Henryson by Hugh MacDiarmid
Herbert by W. H. Auden
Tennyson by Kingsley Amis
Wordsworth by Lawrence Durrell
Whitman by Robert Creeley

Future volumes will include:
Arnold by Stephen Spender
Johnson by Thom Gunn
Marvell by William Empson
Swinburne by I. A. Richards

Poet to Poet

In the introductions to their personal selections from the work of poets they have admired, the individual editors write as follows:

CRABBE SELECTED BY C. DAY LEWIS

'As his poetry displays a balance and decorum in its versification, so his moral ideal is a kind of normality to which every civilized being should aspire. This, when one looks at the desperate expedients and experiments of poets (and others) today, is at least refreshing.'

HERBERT SELECTED BY W. H. AUDEN

'The two English poets, neither of them, perhaps, major poets, whom I would most like to have known well, are William Barnes and George Herbert.

Even if Isaac Walton had never written his life, I think that any reader of his poetry will conclude that George Herbert must have been an exceptionally good man, and exceptionally nice as well.'

TENNYSON SELECTED BY KINSLEY AMIS

'England notoriously had its doubts as well as its certainties, its neuroses as well as its moral health, its fits of gloom and frustration and panic as well as its complacency. Tennyson is the voice of those doubts and their accompaniments, and his genius enabled him to communicate them in such a way that we can understand them and feel them as our own. In short we know from experience just what he means. Eliot called him the saddest of all English poets, and I cannot improve on that judgement.'

The Penguin Book of Scottish Verse

Edited by Tom Scott

This anthology begins with an anonymous poem of the late thirteenth century. However, the history of Scottish poetry goes back much further. As with that of the Irish, it has Gaelic origins. Moreover Scottish literature is written in no less than five languages.

The Penguin Book of Scottish Verse contains only a small, but enticing, section of the poetry which may be claimed as Scottish in the widest sense. It is a selection of poems written in Scots and English, or an amalgam of both, dating from about the 1300s to the present day. To help the general reader unfamiliar with Scottish orthography, the editor has added useful footnotes where necessary, and has tried to standardize the Scots of the pre-Reformation writers without forfeiting the integrity of the poems.

The Penguin Book of Scottish Short Stories

Edited by J. F. Hendry

These twenty stories present a composite picture of the various facets of Scottish writing today. The best of Scottish writing is no mere brew of mists, tartans, and the macabre, but clear, objective, and realistic in spirit: these stories have therefore been selected on a broad basis, without any requirement that they deal with the 'Scottish scene'. By striking a balance between older and younger writers and between stories with a Scottish setting and others (which are no less traditional) the editor has achieved an interesting collection of names as well known as Linklater, Mitchison, and Spark and names which deserve to be better known. One thing is certain: these writers are all Scots.

Poem into Poem
World Poetry in Modern Verse Translation

Edited by George Steiner

Poem into Poem is the only book of its kind – an anthology of verse translations from twenty-two languages, ranging from ancient Hebrew and Greek to modern Chinese. Each translation has been made by an English or American poet who both renders the original and creates what is a living poem in its own right. And what extraordinary encounters result! – Hardy and Sappho, Hopkins and Horace, Yeats and Ronsard, Scott Fitzgerald and Rimbaud, James Joyce and Gottfried Keller, Ezra Pound and Sophocles. The light of another poem is caught in a live mirror.

George Steiner believes that translation is central to the nature of modern poetry: that ours is the most brilliant period of poetic translation and recapture since the Elizabethans. Here is his evidence.

Not for sale in the U.S.A. or Canada